STO

Everyone was looking forward to the weekend and the round of parties for Tom Graham and his bride — everyone except the bride, that is.

For Betty Graham, the return to New York City was bad enough, but the thought of a visit to the socially-minded suburb of Rockton terrified her.

Rockton adjoined its rather shabbier counterpart, the town of Cressland, where three years before one Liz Melinder, purportedly killed in the worst train wreck in years, had escaped her husband and child and set forth for pastures new.

Now, Liz Melinder, alias Betty Graham, felt the multiple threads of her deceit entangling her in a web not necessarily of her own making . . .

Evil is
as Evil Does

by
ROSEMARY GATENBY

M. S. MILL CO., INC.   New York 1967
distributed by
William Morrow & Company, Inc.

Published simultaneously in Canada by
George J. McLeod Limited, Toronto.

Printed in the United States of America.

Library of Congress Catalog Card Number
67-12987

For my husband

1381807

Prologue

It was the worst train wreck of its kind since the Wood-bridge disaster nearly ten years before. Three cars loaded with commuters and Christmas shoppers returning home left the tracks and plunged down an embankment. The train had buckled so that the second coach involved fell on top of the first, twisting the third onto its side. It was a bitter cold evening in December when the days grope through their shortest span, leaving the earth brittle and dark except for a remote scattering of stars. The accident occurred a few minutes before six on a stretch of track about four miles short of Cressland, where a large number of passengers would have gotten off.

It was a nightmare.

A young woman named Liz Melinder was on the train. Having left the baby with her husband's mother that morning, she had escaped just for the day

7

from the hated routine that had held her prisoner since Dickie's birth as surely as Gulliver was held by the ropes of his Lilliputians. Perhaps there were girls who enjoyed making formula, sterilizing bottles, changing diapers, washing all the little soiled garments and hanging them one by one on the line when it was freezing outside or in a tiny bathroom where there was scarcely room to turn around because of the Bathinette. But personally she thought the little mothers who claimed to be happy doing those things were either morons or lying. Or kidding themselves.

Well, she never deluded herself about anything. At least, not any more. The one time she had, she had made a mistake: she had married Al. She had fallen for his big operator line, the sleek cars he drove, the fancy places he took her, and had allowed herself to believe that Al would amount to something. He had been selling cars then, and she had been sure that with his looks and personality he would be a big success, with large commissions and someday an agency of his own. It hadn't worked out that way. He was selling insurance now, not very successfully.

She hadn't wanted the baby, either. Certainly not so soon. But there he was, soiling his didies, spitting up all over himself and her, getting her out of bed at all hours of the night. Most of all, keeping her tied down. She felt as though she'd been given a life sentence, to be served in the kitchen and nursery.

Today in New York had been lovely, even though she had been limited almost entirely to window shopping, Al's finances being what they were these days. Contemplation from the cold, crowded sidewalks of the gorgeously attired and expensively shod mannequins in the windows of Saks Fifth Avenue and Bergdorf's had fanned the flames of her resentment against Al to a sickening heat. Someday, she vowed, she would have a few of the things she wanted. When the baby was bigger she'd arrange something and go back to work. She had been a damn good secretary before she'd had to quit on account of her pregnancy. And for a good secretary there could be all kinds of opportunities . . .

She boarded the 5:03 with the worst crush of commuters. She hadn't taken an earlier train because she couldn't bear to go home until the last possible moment had been squeezed from the day.

As she entered the car the seats were filling up and she slid into the first one available, one on the aisle. If any of her fellow passengers had been paying attention they would have seen quite a pretty dark-haired girl with unusual large brown eyes; protuberant would have described them correctly but ungenerously and would not really have done them justice. The soft curving lips did not really go with the eyes, which an acute observer might have catalogued as rapacious; but then an acute observer would have noticed that the provocative curves of the mouth were painted on outside the

9

natural lines, giving a more pleasant expression than this girl's would actually have been. It was a striking face, a face not easily forgotten once you had seen it.

Liz loosened her coat but did not take it off. It was cold in the train, a clammy cold as it always was when the coaches had been sitting empty in the station. She opened the black suede handbag, the one with the cheap-looking clasp that she hated because Al's mother had given it to her. Having repaired her lipstick she got out her return ticket and stuck it in the slot of the seat-back in front of her. Then she settled back, avoiding the grimy armrest, and looked out through the dirty window. There were a few minutes of dull waiting and then the train pulled out.

The man beside her had folded his paper to the sports page, which didn't interest her, so she glanced around. Executives, these men were—successful. You could tell it by the cut of their clothes, their conservative look. Clothes didn't make the man, but the wrong clothes could certainly put him in his place and keep him there: at the bottom. Al was a prime example, either flashy or sloppy, depending on where he was headed at the moment.

She studied two men diagonally across the aisle. Someone had reversed the seat earlier in the day, probably for a bridge game, and the two sat facing the rear of the train. They were together, the older man by the window. He looked a very wealthy old duck indeed, judging by his hat and overcoat and the briefcase on his lap, and he spoke to his companion with that particular accent which is only to be obtained in a good Eastern prep school.

The younger man looked vaguely familiar, and she examined his well-chiseled profile with quickened interest. He was handsome in a dark, hard-driving way, and almost as well turned out as his companion. Now *there* was the sort of man she should have married. He was discussing sales potentials, quoting production figures, research costs, all on a scale that made Al Melinder and his piddling portfolio of insurance policies look sick. Al probably wouldn't even have known what these men were talking about.

As the man across the aisle turned his head in her direction, Liz's impression that she had seen him somewhere before was confirmed. Harry something, his name was. She smiled, giving him a half nod, but his glance passed over her without an answering glimmer, as though she were a part of the seat. Well, what a snob! In hopes of at least discomfiting him she stared straight at him as he turned again to the older man by the window, but he seemed quite unaware of her existence.

She switched her gaze to the view outside, an endless succession of buildings gliding by, their lights aglow in the early winter dark. Harry Judge, that was his name. And it could be that he didn't even remember her; it was true they had never spoken. He had been ahead of her at Cressland Senior High, a senior the year she started high school—president of the senior class, and one of the lights of the drama club. He'd been off to a good start even then. Obviously he'd been doing well since; he certainly looked the picture of success. Already at—what would he be if he had graduated the year she was a sophomore? Twenty-eight now? She was willing to bet he didn't live in some dumpy house in Cressland, either. He and the other man, too, would live in Rockton, Henning, or one of the other exclusive suburban towns that had grown up beyond Cressland as the commuter tide had reached farther and farther into the countryside.

For most of the trip Liz stared out of the window, bemused.

The train pulled out of the last station before Cressland, where she would be getting off.

"Cr'slud! Cr'slud next!" bawled the conductor and slammed the door behind him.

Al would be meeting her. Thank God at least her mother-in-law would have bathed Dickie and fed him his supper. There was no reason she couldn't stay on at the house while Liz and Al went out to dinner, but Al wouldn't suggest it in a million years. Nowadays he always said they couldn't afford to eat out, but she knew he didn't even want to. He'd rather put on some old greasy pants and a torn, baggy sweater and have dinner at home and watch television. He didn't seem to care about having fun anymore. You never knew when you married them how much they could change later.

When the lurch came it didn't feel like anything more than a rough roadbed for a moment. Then abruptly everything was wrong. Luggage, packages, briefcases came hurtling out of the racks above, striking the passengers below as the floor of the coach tilted at a crazy angle. People were thrown to the floor and then against the windows. The force of gravity seemed to have been suspended as bodies fell up instead of down. The lights flickered and went off, came on, and went out again for good as the coach and its agonized contents hurtled down the slope of the embankment.

Liz felt as if she were on a carnival ride that had somehow gone clear out of control. She hung onto the seat ahead of her with one hand and to the luggage rack above with the other.

And then the motion and the buffeting stopped. To ease her aching arm, she let go of the luggage rack, losing her balance in so doing, and she half slid, half fell across the aisle. The coach, she saw, lay partly on its side—not the side she had been sitting on, the other one. The front end was sharply downhill from the rear. Faint light from somewhere came through the windows, enough to show the jumbled shapes of people trying to extricate themselves from the seats. A few lay still or moving feebly, but most were looking about to see what had happened, and then disentangling themselves from their traveling companions and trying to find a way to climb up towards the rear door.

Liz was braced against the seat across the aisle. In the dim light she could see the rich old duck huddled in the corner. Blood ran down his forehead and he seemed dazed.

"Help me up, will you? Someone—"

Liz compressed her lips and laboriously made her way past him. All around her, and especially from the front end of the car which lay downhill, were sounds of distress, with here and there a plea for help. "My God, oh my God, oh my God!" one woman repeated over and over. Well, there were others who could help; it wasn't her job.

"This way! Out this way!" a man by the rear door called in a clear, confident voice. Liz could see him handing people over the threshold as they succeeded in getting that far. She made her way up the slanting floor, hanging onto each seat as she progressed, and at last reached the exit. With a firm hand the man at the door helped her up and out.

The car was tilted so that there was at least a four-foot drop to the ground, but she made it easily, turning her ankle rather painfully as she landed askew on one high heel.

She had been lucky, she saw, to be in this coach, not the two ahead of it, which lay twisted and intertwined, one on top of the other. She shuddered. The people in there—she couldn't see very well in the darkness but it looked bad, very bad.

A man carrying a railroad lantern stopped at her side and looked her over. "You all right, Miss?"

"Yes. Of course I'm all right."

The man went on. But in the beam of his light she had seen the dark, sticky blood matting the suede of her handbag. She hadn't known she still had it in her hand. It wasn't her blood, she was sure. She felt in the bag for a handkerchief to wipe it off.

"Could of been us," said a voice at her elbow. She hadn't noticed the woman, but now she saw her standing there, staring at the crumpled coaches. "Could of been you or me."

"Yes. Yes, it could." Liz resumed her search for a handkerchief as the woman moved away down the embankment. Sirens wailed now in the distance, more than one. Coming here. Men, running to help, were crossing the dark ground from a factory building nearby. The factory lights cast almost the only illumination available as yet on the disaster.

Her eyes went back to the mangled wreckage which lay below. No one had gotten out of those two cars. Not yet anyway. Maybe there wasn't anyone alive in there. Could have been me, she thought again.

And then she stopped looking for the handkerchief. She must think very carefully.

With an unexpected surge of pleasure she thought of Al waiting for her at the station. Waiting for her and she wouldn't be there. She thought how it would be never to see Al again. Or the baby.

She thought of her clothes hanging at home in the closet. Rags, practically. Nothing to go back for.

A cold, thrilling exaltation swept over her like a shot of some strange drug. She felt suddenly changed: her blood ran faster, her thoughts formed more clearly. She saw everything with a beautiful icy clarity. She felt no doubt about what she must do.

She gazed coldly and carefully at the two dreadful, lifeless coaches, with men from the rest of the train and from the factory milling about them now. The people in there must be mincemeat. Hard to identify.

In the darkness she felt in her handbag for her wallet and took out the money. Not much there, but it would have to do. She dropped the wallet back in. She groped for her lipstick, found it, but thought again and put it back. She'd buy a new one. She snapped shut the ugly clasp. Anywhere would do, she supposed. She hurled the bloody handbag into the darkness under the coach she had left.

Seized by excitement such as she had never felt, she turned from the scene and started walking in the opposite direction from the rescue operations, back along the tracks. Even the pain in her ankle gave her a sense of exultation. She could feel it, but it didn't hurt. She felt larger than life. Like the people you saw in wide-screen movies.

"Oh, yes, one more thing!" she whispered to herself. In one quick motion she had taken off her wedding ring and flung it onto the tracks. She was disappointed not to hear it fall. But she knew that it lay there, somewhere between the ties, with the initials inscribed on the inside, "A. T. M. to E. A. M."

She walked on along the ties in the darkness, not even aware of the bitter cold.

Chapter 1

TOM GRAHAM stood at the window of their hotel suite looking out at the green of Central Park. It was a hot day, as he knew from the morning paper, but you couldn't tell it in here because of the air-conditioning.

He was perplexed.

Of course he had known Betty was upset over the transfer to New York, and he could understand that. She had been unhappy here as a child. But he had been sure that once they were settled things would be all right. New York when you had money was not the same city that the poor lived in. The Grahams would have a nice apartment, or a house in the suburbs, and good friends, because Tom had made lots of friends when he'd lived here before. They would go to the theater, concerts, the best restaurants, which of course would be all new to Betty. She need never go near the old neighborhood in the Bronx which she had always been reluctant even to mention.

He had been sure that when she got to know his New York she would like it. But it didn't seem to be turning out that way. She remained as nervous as a cat and evil tempered to a degree he had not before experienced in the ten months of their marriage. Even the invitation for the weekend. He had thought she'd be pleased because at least for a couple of days they'd be getting away from the city, but it seemed only to have made matters worse. She didn't like his accepting the invitation without consulting her.

He turned from the window to watch his wife as she sat at the desk carefully applying nail polish, her blonde head bent over her labors.

"You'll have a good time once we're there. I know you will," he said hopefully.

"Just like I'm having a good time in New York. You said I would."

"I wish you wouldn't be so sarcastic. I can't help it about New York; we've been over that enough times. My job is here now. And I'm still sure you'll like it when you get used to it."

"I'm trying, Tom, really I am." She looked up at him with those tremendous brown eyes. "You just don't realize how a dreadful childhood can warp your whole outlook about some things. You've never been poor, shoved around, unwanted. You don't know what it's like to live in a foster home."

"No, of course I don't." As always when she said things like that, he felt a stab of pity, and the accompanying uneasy stirrings of guilt because he himself had never known poverty or emotional want.

"Well, you don't get over it in a day. Or a year." She did the little finger of her left hand and shifted the brush to do the other hand.

"Yes, I know, darling. I realize it's not easy for you."

"It was easy enough in Chicago. I felt I'd gotten far enough away. I was a new me. But here—it all comes back."

He crossed the room to stand beside her and dropped a kiss on her forehead.

"That's why I thought you'd welcome a chance to get away for the weekend, anyhow, to the country. When Marcia called—"

Betty gave a tight little smile. "Well, we're stuck with it now, anyway, since you accepted. Where did you say they live?"

"Rockton."

"Oh, yes." She paused, then dipped the brush in the bottle again and lacquered the last nail. "Oh, damn! I've spoiled it!"

She had to take the polish off that one and do it over.

"They were very good friends of yours at one time, didn't you tell me?"

"Jim and Marcia? Oh, God yes! Jim and I were friends at college. Then when we were both working here in New York we used to see a lot of each other—till he married Marcia. After that, of course, it wasn't as often, and finally they bought a house and moved out. But I still saw them on weekends, even then. They asked me out quite frequently."

"Marcia wasn't an old girl friend of yours, was she? Jim cut you out or something?" Betty looked up slantwise at him.

"God, no! I'm girl-shy, always have been. I've told you."

Betty stood up and slid her arms around the neck of the tall, sandy-haired young man.

"You weren't shy with *me!*"

"You were different."

"Was I? I'm glad." Her eyes were soft and luminous, her lips a half-open invitation to anything he might desire. He was sure she didn't know how seductive she was when she looked like that. No nice girl would do it on purpose—even with her own husband. Or would she? He still didn't understand women; in fact he understood them even less, it seemed, since he had married.

Chapter 2

BETTY GRAHAM stood before the mirror in Marcia Townsend's guest room repairing her lipstick and re-etching her eyebrows. She was careful with the reshaping of her upper lip, going outside the natural lines but with the fullness extended out towards the corners instead of near the center in the cupid's bow she used to fashion. The lower lip was easy; she only had to emphasize it with a swipe of color—full and a little pouting. Her eyebrows were full, too, instead of the delicately plucked arches they had been three years before. Altogether she liked her new face much better than the old one. She thought it even had more character. And the T.V. commercials were right: it *was* more fun to be a blonde.

Thank heavens they had driven out from New York. To have taken the train to Cressland would have been a greater strain on her composure than she was prepared to risk. They could so easily have run into someone she knew. Now that they were actually at Rockton she felt relatively safe. It might be only five miles from Cressland, but socially it was another world. This was where the rich lived, on the wooded hills overlooking the Sound. None of her old friends, none of Al's, even knew anyone in Rockton. And none of them knew the girl in the mirror. She was Betty Graham of Chicago. Liz Melinder had died in a train wreck three years ago. Yet standing here only a few minutes' drive from the hateful little house she had lived in with Al Melinder, she found it difficult to remember that there was no more Liz. Her old identity kept slipping insidiously over the new, blotting out the person she had become since she went away.

It was true, what she had said to Tom. Being in New York brought everything back, everything she thought she had left behind her: not the orphaned Bronx childhood she told Tom about, a fiction which conveniently explained her lack of family or other ties; but the ordinary girlhood, with ordinary parents like everyone else's, and lots of friends who unfortunately still lived around here.

She thought again how lucky it was that at least she ran no risk of coming face to face with Mom and Dad in this neck of the woods. A girl's own mother would, of course, be bound to recognize her. It was nice to know they were safely in Florida, where they had moved when Dad retired not long after Betty and Al were married. They lived down there in one of those "golden age" villages.

But the worst thing of all, the knowledge from which she could not turn away, was that she was still legally married to Albert Treadly Melinder, who lived at 23 Apple Lane, Cressland, and that she was the mother of his four-year-old son.

Until now she had not really felt that she was living a stolen life. In Chicago she had felt truly married to Tom; she had been safe and happy, married at last to the kind of man she should have held out for in the first place. But since the day they had arrived in New York she had been almost afraid to turn around for fear she would find Al following her, Al ready to reach out and take her by the shoulder and say, "Hey, look, you're *my* wife!"

"Good God, where's your motorcycle?" Tom had exclaimed when he first caught sight of her wearing the wraparound sunglasses. She had bought them the day they arrived.

"They're the style," she had said, too sharply. "If you read the fashion magazines you'd know that." And she hoped he didn't really wonder about them.

Well, she shouldn't worry about this evening, she knew. "Just a few neighbors," Marcia had said of the dinner guests who would be coming. "People Tom used to know."

Marcia was a long-stemmed American Beauty, about thirty or so and the mother of two. Her pleasure in welcoming Betty was genuine. They'd been trying for years to marry Tom off, she remarked, but now she was glad he had waited for the right girl. Quite the correct thing to say, thought Betty. She and Marcia would get along fine.

Tom had gone on downstairs in hopes that Jim had arrived home by now. Marcia said he would be taking an early train, today being Friday. Betty was almost ready. She slipped the diamond watch Tom had given her from its case and put it on. Tom really was a marvelous husband. Everything she could ever have wanted!

With a final satisfied look in the mirror she left the guest room and went down the carpeted stairway to join the party.

"And this must be the bride!" Jim Townsend rose from the sofa at the far end of the large, beige-colored living room where he had sat talking with Marcia and Tom. He was a big hulk of a man, pleasant looking, whose bulk and movements equally proclaimed him a former college football player. He advanced and took Betty's hand as she came down the steps from the front hall. "Why, she's a beauty, Tom. You did very well without our help." He led her over to the others. "Welcome to our group, Betty. We've been waiting a long time for Tom to even things up and make us a four-some."

She took a seat next to Tom, where she could hold his hand.

"What'll you have to drink? Martini? Manhattan?"

"A martini's fine."

That's lucky, thought Marcia, eyeing the tremendous pitcher of cocktails mixed and ready on the marble coffee table. If Tom and Jim didn't have considerable help on downing all that they'd both be boiled. She knew them of old.

Marcia smiled at Betty in friendly fashion. The girl seemed hesitant, which surprised her because she'd been very self-possessed when they arrived earlier in the afternoon. Perhaps it was hard for her, meeting Tom's old friends and wondering whether they would like her. She must do her best to make Betty feel one of them from the start.

"We hope to persuade you and Tom to move out around here," Marcia began.

"That's nice of you," Betty said carefully. "It's beautiful here, of course. And I love your house." She glanced admiringly around the big room furnished in what she recognized as French Provincial. The house itself was French in style, too, she thought; she remembered that the exterior was white and very elegant. She was trying to learn about such things because it was important to know them. People at this economic level automatically knew style and period; they had grown up with it and they spent their money on it. They knew real from fake.

"We can find you a place out here, no trouble at all," offered Jim. "Marcia can take you around and introduce you to the real estate people—"

"Oh, no, thanks, not yet." Betty protested lightly. "I'm still learning to cook; I don't know what I'd do with a house!"

Tom put his arm around her. "Betty wants an apartment, just for now. Right, darling?"

"You mean live in New York?" Jim shook his head. "No one lives in New York. At least not until they get too old to commute, or unless they have an apartment in town *and* a place in the country. You're crazy!"

"Jim!" said Marcia. "What's the matter with you? They're newlyweds. Why should they need a house?"

"Newlyweds! God. That seems like a long time ago, doesn't it, Marcia?"

"Well, you needn't sound so awestruck! It's only been eight years, and I'm not even touching up my hair yet, though you may have given me cause!"

"They bite when they get older," Jim explained. "Though you haven't that problem yet, Tom. I hope you're treating yours right. Any complaints?" He turned to Betty.

"Oh, I'm saving those for the big payoff, when I decide to ask for my mink." She looked up at Tom and squeezed his hand.

Marcia tried again to feel that she was really going

27

to like Betty. She turned to Tom. "By the way, you re-member Karen and Harry, I'm sure? They're coming this evening."

"Harry Judge! Yes, indeed."

Nothing more than a polite glaze of interest showed on Betty's face, but for a moment the muscles in her stomach tensed at the familiar name. Harry Judge. Someone who had, evidently, made the transition from Cressland to Rockton.

"Who are they? The Judges?" she asked, sipping her drink. Harry wouldn't remember her, of that she was sure. He hadn't remembered her that day on the train, and she hadn't really changed so much then; he would never connect her, now, with a green kid he'd never even noticed when he was at Cressland High.

"They live just down the road," Tom was explain-ing. "I used to play a lot of bridge with them when I came out here weekends."

"I guess they'd just been married, then, hadn't they —the year before you went away?" Marcia was thought-ful. "Seems like quite a while ago."

"Nice girl, Karen. How's Harry been?"

"Prospering," said Jim. "Prospering. He's got it made, of course, ever since Karen's father was killed. You remember he stepped in as head of Kendrick Com-pany."

Tom nodded. "I remember. I was East on a business trip not long after it happened. I remember being out here and talking to Harry. I'd read about the accident in the Chicago papers, of course. Terrible thing!"

He broke off as the living room was invaded by two small children, a boy and a girl in shorts and tee-shirts.

She doesn't like children, thought Marcia as Betty pulled her skirt more closely about her knees and edged over away from them on the sofa, a smile on her lips but panic in her eyes.

Their stay was brief. "Run along, now—both of you. Mrs. Wiebald must be nearly ready to give you your supper."

For Betty her words, so unexpected, tolled with the clangor of an alarm bell. She sat quite still. Mrs. Wiebald. On two or three occasions when Al's mother couldn't come to mind Dickie they had hired a sitter. Her name was Mrs. Wiebald.

"When we have a party we usually get a sitter to come in and keep Tim and Suzie out of our hair and the guests' laps. They love to be in the middle of things."

Betty scarcely heard what Marcia was saying as the Townsend offspring disappeared out into the hall and clattered towards the rear of the house. The name could be a coincidence—but unnerving, to be sure, coming so soon after the news that an old schoolmate would be among those present this evening. She mustn't let such little surprises upset her. Besides, Mrs. Wiebald, whoever she was, was certainly not joining the party in the living room.

"They're darling children," she forced herself to say. It was easier to think so now that the little dears had gone.

"Thank you." Marcia's level gaze met hers.

The first of the guests was arriving. They heard a car door slam.

"It's Quint," said Jim from the window.

"Oh," said Marcia. "Yes, I invited him for Jeannie." She broke off and turned to Betty. "You haven't met Jeannie yet."

"No." Who was Jeannie?

"Quincy Rutledge?" Tom seemed startled.

"What a marvelous name," murmured Betty. Like someone in a six hundred page southern novel, she thought.

"Yes, isn't it!" agreed her host. "And it suits him. He's a lawyer, believe it or not. Man with a name like that would be sure to get you off. He's built his reputation just on the sound of it."

Quincy Rutledge looked as impressive as his name. Betty watched him cross the room, tall and alert, a look of brilliance about him, an impression conveyed immediately by the quick, lean face and discerning eyes. Nearly fifty he looked to be, though as fit as a much younger man.

"Quint, you old dog!" Jim clapped him on the shoulder and brought him towards Betty and Tom. "Come and greet the guests of honor."

When Quint took her hand and bowed slightly over it Betty felt uncomfortable in some unaccountable way, as if her dress were too low or a zipper had slipped.

Tom he knew, and the two of them talked agreeably for some time, but when Quint's attention returned to her, Betty fared no better than before. As they conversed he stared unswervingly at her with keen eyes, greenish in hue and with an odd trick of contracting the lower lids every few moments in a kind of squint. She came to feel as if he could read her mind; it became harder and harder to smile and speak naturally.

Marcia's voice floated in to them from the foyer. "Karen! Come in! How are you, Harry?" Betty's eyes were drawn in avid curiosity to the other end of the room as Karen and Harry Judge appeared, talking to their hostess.

She would hardly have known Harry Judge. He had changed. He seemed to have put on weight. He was not actually fat, strangely, except around the face. It was as though his straight, handsome features had become embedded in an agglomeration of fleshy tissue until now they were well-nigh unrecognizable. Dissipation probably accounted for it, for he still looked relatively young. He could not, in fact, be much over thirty.

Karen Judge she dismissed at a glance. A nothing. Money, obviously, as her beautifully made but casual dress and expensive shoes clearly indicated. But she was so plain it was almost a sin, and from the look on her face, used to letting everyone walk right over her. It was surprising, then, that Quint Rutledge took such an interest in her from the moment she entered the room. Her money? thought Betty. Perhaps. Yet a financial interest did not explain the warmth in his face that had not been there until she came.

Other people were arriving now and the party began to spread out. Quint drifted away from Betty and someone buttonholed Tom and took him off to one side.

Harry Judge, having procured a highball for himself, lost no time in devoting his full attention to Betty. He looked warmly and admiringly down into her eyes.

"I'm sure we've met before."

It was such an old and obvious line that she almost laughed in his face, but managed to smile engagingly instead. Apparently Harry would rather start from first base than from the plate.

"Oh, now, that one's *much* too old! You know we haven't met."

"We haven't?" He sounded a bit blank. He must like to seem sincere. "Well, that situation's been remedied then, hasn't it! So you're the little bride we've been hearing about."

"Not quite a bride, by now. It's been almost a year."

His eyes crinkled. "The honeymoon is over, then."

"I didn't say that."

Tom was beside her again.

"You can't trust Harry at all with a pretty girl," he warned her, slipping a proprietary arm about her waist.

"Get lost, boy. We were just getting acquainted. Now you've spoiled it."

"How've you been, Harry?"

"Can't complain."

"How's business?"

"Great. I've got the whole shebang to run now, you know."

"So I heard. A terrible thing about Karen's father."

"Yes, wasn't it." But Harry's attention did not seem to be fully engaged in discussing whatever unkind fate had overtaken his wife's father. He was still ogling Betty.

Tom's eyes rested on Harry's wife, who stood near them talking to Quint Rutledge. "It must have been very rough on Karen."

"Yes. She and her father were always very close. Poor kid."

Betty's attention drifted off as the conversation got bogged down in the affairs of the Kendrick Company. Why did men always have to talk shop? Luckily Marcia came and fetched her away to introduce her to some people she hadn't met—Chuck Bennett, a short, dapper young man, and his gabby, bosomy wife. Someone brought her another drink. With the added guests the noise level rose, compliments flowed, people laughed, and suddenly she found that she was really enjoying herself. A uniformed maid was passing canapés. *That's not Mrs. Wiebald at least,* she noted, observing the woman out of the corner of her eye. But then a sitter wouldn't be wearing a uniform or passing food; get her out of your mind, she told herself.

It was at this moment that she saw the girl descending the curved stairs in the front hall. A beautiful girl. She was not one of the guests who had left the party to go upstairs, because if she had been in the living room at all Betty would have seen her. "You haven't met Jeannie," Marcia had said earlier, seeming to refer to a member of the household, and Betty had wondered whom she meant. This, then, must be Jeannie.

The girl crossed the hall and paused to survey the guests.

She was young, not much more than twenty. The sweep of almost straight blonde hair was streaked from sun and water, and the lovely blue eyes were intensified by the deep tan of her skin. She seemed to be looking for someone. And then it was obvious she had found him. Swiftly she came down the two steps from the hall and made her way across the room. To Tom.

Tom.

Now what was *that* about? He lit up like a Christmas tree when he caught sight of her and kissed her soundly when she reached his side. Girl-shy? Indeed!

And then he was bringing her across the room to Betty, his arm about the slim, tanned shoulders.

"Betty, this is Jeannie Townsend, Jim's sister. My wife, Jeannie."

Betty took in this vision of loveliness with all the natural affection of the artificial blonde for the genuine. With her best party manner she smiled.

"How do you do, Jeannie." She managed to make the name sound childishly young, but spoke with such an air of friendliness that the girl couldn't have taken offense. "Do you know, Tom never told me Jim had a sister. Now I can see why. He was afraid to; you're much too attractive!" She smiled up at Tom, as much as to say he was a sly old dog.

Such remarks always threw Tom into confusion. He didn't know whether he was expected to laugh it off or defend himself.

Jeannie spoke for him. "If Tom never mentioned me it was for the very good reason that he never gave me a thought. I was just a kid the last time he saw me: fifteen and hopelessly stringy."

"All wrapped up in girl scouting, as I recall," said Tom.

"I haven't changed much either, I guess. I'm working this summer as a counselor at a day camp. That's why I'm a little late to the party—it's a fair drive home from the camp."

Quint Rutledge was watching this little exchange from nearby, reading faces instead of following the words very closely. It was almost like watching Pearl

35

White being fed into a buzz saw, except that Jeannie could take care of herself pretty well. He doubted that Tom was as capable. If he had been, he'd never have gotten himself married to such a girl. A vicious piece if he'd ever seen one. Too bad, too. He liked Tom. Some men just had no sense about women at all; they could be taken in by the worst kind of shoddy merchandise. Of course it worked both ways, too; many a time a girl, especially one with money . . . but then it was no use thinking of that any more.

He moved forward to rescue Jeannie. He would be doing Tom a favor, too; if he could read the signs, the beleaguered bridegroom would only get himself into trouble between the two of them.

Dinner was served buffet style on the screened terrace in back.

"Where's Jim?" Tom asked Marcia as he came face to face with her on his way back for a second helping.

"Don't ask." She looked slightly embarrassed. "He's passed out. I put him in the den."

"Would you like me to go and look in on him?"

"Oh, I think he's all right, thanks. He doesn't do this often. Just when he gets carried away."

"Carried out, don't you mean?" Tom smiled. "It's happened to me plenty of times, as you know."

"But maybe you've learned, by now. Neither age nor

experience has ever taught Jim that martinis are stronger than he is."

Tom gave her a pat on the shoulder. "I'll go see how he is."

Harry Judge was still hovering around Betty, eyeing her knowingly and making what seemed rather leading remarks. He must really like to play the field, and, Betty concluded, with apparently no thought as to what his wife might feel. But then she was so plain she probably felt thankful to have gotten married at all.

Harry was really not bad looking, she was thinking, in spite of the fat around his face.

He was smiling at her, with a wise gleam in his eye. "How did a simple soul like Tom ever latch on to a hep doll like you?"

"Oh, Tom's not simple. Don't you believe it!"

"That's not what I meant. I know he's a bright guy —brilliant, actually. But unsophisticated."

"That kind make the best husbands."

"You bet. One hundred percent domestic and trustworthy as all hell. I'm afraid I'm not that kind."

"So I thought." Her large, fascinating brown eyes glowed with slight amusement and, he thought, something like interest.

"I don't believe in being tied down." He spoke slowly and carefully, looking at her. "Let my wife be tied down." This was a damn good-looking girl, and one with not too many scruples, he was sure. And again he had the feeling that he had seen her before.

"Here, Betty, let me take that for you." He reached for her empty plate, to dispose of it along with his. Someone jostled him from behind. "Oh, I'm sorry!" Salad dressing dribbled down the front of her skirt.

"It's nothing," she said, sounding annoyed nevertheless. "I'll go and sponge it off."

"Oh, dear!" Marcia came over to them. "Can I fix that for you, Betty?"

"Thanks, I just need a dab of cold water—"

"The powder room, then. Right under the stairs."

Harry finished his cigarette and then followed her. Not with any great speed, he just wandered in the direction of the front hall so that he could reclaim her when she came out. She was the lushest thing to come his way in some time, and he didn't want anyone else getting ahead of him. Not that he thought for even a moment that she was ready to plunge into an affair, or anything bordering it. Not yet. But she'd be fun to play around with a little. Surely before long she'd be getting bored with that husband of hers: Tom was a man's man, he couldn't have much to offer to the ladies, of that he was sure. And when boredom set in, good old Harry Judge would have the inside track.

Behind the broad spread of stairs which curved down into the middle of the large foyer were two doors. One was that of the powder room, the other opened on the hall from the kitchen and back part of the house. Wall sconces lit the back part of the hall, but only dimly. A brighter light came from the ceiling of the stairwell, lighting the steps from the second floor.

As Harry stood in the near end of the deserted, half-dark living room, a waspish-looking female in her middle years descended the steps. He recognized her as the sitter, and only half glanced at her before turning partly away; he wasn't going to get caught in a conversation with *this* old bag! She reached the bottom of the stairs and headed for the hall door. Harry turned back just in time to see the door to the powder room swing open and the light switch off. There was a gasp and then silence. Betty stood in the half-open doorway, her hair in shadow so that it looked dark, not blonde. Her face was as though turned to stone, the protuberant eyes fixed on the woman before her, whose back was now to Harry.

"Mrs. Melinder! Why, you are! Mrs. Albert Melinder. Oh, yes!" She pushed the girl back into the tiny room and turned on the light so that it flooded down on the golden hair.

Betty narrowed her eyes and smiled coldly. Harry could see the two of them in the little room as though it were a lighted stage set. They were talking in profile to him now and he could no longer hear what was said. Something like a momentary doubt seemed to come into the older woman's face as she studied the light hair, the slitted eyes, and the stony poise of the other. Then she pressed her lips together, apparently more certain than ever.

Betty snapped off the light and came out. ". . . very upsetting if it weren't so patently ridiculous!" He caught the last of her words.

The sitter's face was fiery red by now. She wrenched open the other door, the one to the back regions, and turned for one parting shot.

"I was over to your house last week, too: sitting with your Dickie. Looks just like you. Even the blonde hair. *Exactly* like you, Mrs. Melinder. Only *he's* a natural human being, not like his mother, whatever she is! Poor little tyke!" Her face twisted as though she were about to cry and she slammed the door.

Harry moved away. He hardly wanted to take up his conversation with Betty just now, even if she were ready to, which seemed highly improbable.

He needed time to digest what he had witnessed.

No one else had observed this fascinating little drama. The living room was empty, everyone being out on the terrace. Harry went over to the antique cabinet where he knew Jim kept a decanter of brandy and poured himself a drink. He sat down near one of the front windows of the darkened room. It had been still light when the party had moved outside, and he guessed no one had thought to turn on the lights in here.

Rolling the glass between his palms to bring out by

their warmth the bouquet of the brandy, he gazed through the panes of leaded glass without really seeing the dark shapes of the cars parked in the circle of the turn-around that swept past the front door and turned back upon itself in the inky shadows of the trees at the other end of the house. The grass and the evergreens this side of the drive, and the rhododendron flanking the living room bay window shone a bright unnatural green in the illumination from spotlights in the eaves, making everything beyond them, by contrast, doubly dark.

For some little time Harry Judge sat there in the living room, alone with his drink, his thoughts on the past and its bearing on the here and now.

And then, almost as though his thoughts had placed her there, where he could see her, Betty appeared out on the lawn. Through the glass of the window where he sat he could see her as she emerged quickly from the ornamental trees by the front door onto a patch of grass illuminated by one of the spotlights. As quickly, she went on into another clump of trees by the drive. It was not surprising, he thought, that she had felt no inclination to rejoin the party immediately. But what was she doing out there?

And what would she do, he wondered as he got to his feet, if the baby-sitter told all? Brazen it out?

Chapter 3

MRS. WIEBALD paused in the back hallway after slamming the door behind her.

"Well, I *never!*" she exclaimed to herself. "And bold as brass she was, too."

She went on into the kitchen in time to see Marcia Townsend starting for the dining room with a large serving tray laden with gold-edged coffee cups and saucers and a fan of heavy silver spoons.

"Oh, you're ready to leave?" Marcia set the tray down on the counter.

"Yes. Suzie and Tim are both in bed. I read them a couple of stories and waited a little to make sure they were asleep." Mrs. Wiebald was still frowning over that encounter just now under the front stairway. But Marcia didn't notice; she was looking up at the wall clock and computing Mrs. Wiebald's pay: almost a quarter to nine. From a drawer where she kept ready cash she took out a sheaf of bills and peeled off four which she handed to the baby-sitter.

Mrs. Wiebald hesitated, studying the money in her hand as though she had never before seen the face of George Washington.

"Thank you, Mrs. Wiebald. And we'll see you again tomorrow." Marcia picked up the coffee tray and backed with it toward the door leading to the dining room and terrace.

"Mrs. Townsend," began the sitter, at last taking her wallet from the purse she carried and stuffing the money into it, "I—"

But her employer had vanished from the kitchen and Gertrude Wiebald was left standing there with her mouth open. Now she closed it, and dropping the wallet back into the handbag, closed that, too.

She had started for the outside door, which opened onto the back walk, when the dining-room door swung in, bringing with it Jeannie Townsend.

"Leaving us, Mrs. Wiebald? Little imps tucked in, I expect." She went to the cabinet where the everyday china was kept. "*Large* cup," she murmured to herself as she opened the door and peered within. "Oh, dear!"

"*There's* one." From the center of the room Mrs. Wiebald could see a king-sized cup in back of the others on the upper shelf. She reached over Jeannie's head to lift it down.

"Oh, thanks! Should be big enough, shouldn't it!"

Jeannie picked up the percolator and poured out a full cup.

"Jeannie," said Mrs. Wiebald, "that blonde lady with the big brown eyes. Who is she?"

"That's Mrs. Graham, our house guest." She answered rather absently, wondering if Jim would be able to drink the coffee by now if she took it in to him.

"Have you known her long?"

"Why, no." Suddenly Jeannie's attention was fully on the conversation. Why should Mrs. Wiebald be interested in Betty Graham? "She and Mr. Graham just moved here from Chicago. She—"

Jeannie broke off as she realized that the door from the back hall had opened and the subject of their discussion stood right there listening. She could have sunk through the floor. Surely Betty wouldn't really think she had been discussing her with the help. She hadn't meant to, only she just hadn't been paying attention when Mrs. Wiebald started in.

"Oh," said Betty. "Hello Jeannie." She nodded to Mrs. Wiebald. Her hand on the knob of the open door, she hesitated. "You haven't seen Tom anywhere have you?"

"Not lately. Why don't you try the terrace?" Jeannie suggested.

Betty's gaze shifted to Mrs. Wiebald, with what seemed to be an effort at a smile. "This little lady assures me I look like someone she used to know. Has she been telling you?"

"Why, no. That is . . ." Jeannie groped for the right thing to say. This should be an opportunity to explain away the conversation Betty must have overheard. But before she could finish Mrs. Wiebald broke in.

"I'll be going now. Tell your sister-in-law I'll be seeing *her* again tomorrow." She looked past Jeannie to the figure in the doorway, and in her voice was an odd, determined quality. Gertrude Wiebald drew her green fishnet sweater about her, slung her purse on her arm by its strap, and took her departure by way of the back kitchen entry.

Jeannie stared after her, puzzled by what struck her as a peculiarly abrupt change of manner. Usually you could hardly get the woman out the door she was so talkative—and always friendly. Now she had suddenly shut up like a clam and twice as chilly. Jeannie shrugged and turned back to Betty, only to find that that door, too, had closed and she was alone in the kitchen.

Betty went swiftly through the front hall and out the wide door, which stood open.

Now which way had the woman gone? Out the back door, but she'd have to come around the front to the drive. Yes, there she was. Betty caught sight of her

45

walking out the drive towards the road—a dark form barely discernible against the leafy blackness beyond the parked cars. Quickly she left the shelter of the trees by the front door, cut across a lighted patch of lawn and through the trees again to catch up with the receding figure. As she went, she slipped her diamond watch from her wrist.

The coffee would be cold now. Jeannie dumped it out and poured a fresh cup, her thoughts as dark and bitter as the brew.

As yet she had only a premonition of disaster. No, more than that: it was a certainty of disaster to come that she felt. Two hours ago it had been a premonition, when she first took Tom's hand and he leaned over and kissed her. Her feelings had progressed apace since then and she had been powerless to stop them.

How could she not have known? The surprise of it was complete. She had, of course, not forgotten her schoolgirl crush on him; but she had thought of it as just that, and had supposed that when they met again she would wonder what she had found so divine about him when she was fifteen. She could have filled a large scrapbook with the pictures of the teenage crushes she had outgrown, one, two, and even three at a time. But Tom was another matter, and she hadn't known it.

Jeannie Townsend—in love with a married man?

She would have thought it impossible. Maybe she was feverish, coming down with something.

She'd better get this coffee to Jim before it got cold, too.

"Jim!" She opened the door to the den and crossed the room where she stood by the leather sofa looking down at the supine hulk of her brother. "Jim wake up."

He opened one eye and shut it again.

"Jim, I've brought you some coffee. Sit up and drink it." She set it down on the end table and then went to work trying to hoist him up to a sitting position. Halfway there he opened both eyes and eased himself into an upright slouch. He rubbed his face with both hands.

"Why coffee? I haven't had dinner yet."

"Dinner's over."

He squinted up at her in distress. "Dinner's *over?*" She nodded. "Oh, no! I didn't do *that* again!" He shook his head, though not very hard as it might have made him dizzy. He turned to stare at the coffee. "Thanks. Run along, now. I'll drink it. Really I will."

"I'll be back after awhile."

As the door closed behind her he slumped back on the couch and shut his eyes.

Bleak unhappiness claimed Jeannie. Moving in a fog of murky thoughts she retraced her steps to the kitchen. It was empty, and she lingered there a few minutes, reluctant to return to the gaiety of the party. Oh, this will never do! she thought, and tried to shake off her mood.

She didn't know whether to be glad or not a little later, when she met Tom coming towards her at the bottom of the stairs in the foyer.

"Hi." She caught hold of the newel post and was careful not to stand too close to him.

"I was just going to check on Jim again."

"He's trying to come to. I took him some coffee."

"Do you think he'd eat something if we brought it?"

She shook her head. "Might make him sick. Poor Jim! He doesn't do this often. Really!"

"Just what Marcia said. We wouldn't know good old Jim if he didn't pull this once in awhile, I guess."

"At least, as he says himself, he's always a cheerful drunk. The life of the party until he blacks out."

Tom laughed. "He does do that, doesn't he! Blotto. I remember some of us at the fraternity house used to kid the hell out of him telling him things he'd done the night before after a few drinks. We could tell him anything, because he couldn't remember. Made his life miserable on a few occasions."

"And you call yourself a friend?"

"He did things as bad to me. Worse. The good old days. You went to K. U. too, didn't you?"

"Yes. Family tradition. Dad went there, you know."

"You must have finished now?"

"Just. I got my degree in June."

"Ah. A mere child." He shook his head.

She smiled, and Tom thought again what an enchanting girl this child had turned into. Perhaps he was getting used to women at last, after all, because he felt perfectly at home with Jeannie. Ordinarily he was tongue-tied in the presence of females.

"At least," she said, "you didn't tell me I'd grown."

"No. But I'm afraid I raised an eyebrow when I heard you were going with Quint. He seems a trifle old for you. I trust you're not—engaged to him or anything?"

In spite of her good intentions she savored a small, grateful pleasure in Tom's look of worry. He cared a little about her then; anything less would, she felt, be unbearable.

"No, I'm not engaged to Quint. I'm not 'going' with him, even. Marcia likes even numbers at her parties; you know how it is in the married set. All my friends have scattered since I went off to college, of course; I hardly know anyone my age around here now. So Quint's convenient. Poor guy. He's never dated anyone seriously since Karen Kendrick, you know. It was such a shame that Harry cut him out."

"I take it you don't like Harry."

Her eyes glinted. "No, as a matter of fact I don't. He's given Karen a rotten time, and she's such a dear." She broke off. "I think Betty's looking for you."

49

Betty was coming towards them through the living room. The lights were on in there now and a few people had drifted back in from the terrace.

She looked deathly pale.

"What is it?" Tom took her arm. "Don't you feel well?"

She let out a long, shaky breath. Her eyes looked almost glazed. "I'll be all right. Hold onto me. Just a touch of—something."

"Here. We'll sit on the steps." He pulled her down beside him on the carpeted stair tread.

She shook her head to Jeannie's offers of assistance. "I'll be all right in a minute. Really."

"Well, if you want anything . . ."

As Jeannie left them, Tom pressed Betty against his shoulder.

"What's wrong, darling? Headache or something?"

She looked up at him wanly, but with tenderness. "Maybe I'm pregnant," she said. That should get him.

He beamed.

She wasn't, she knew; but men were so stupid about all that. And such suckers for the son and heir. She might just stick with that story for awhile.

Just as it was starting to break up, Jim made it back to the party. He had to take a little ribbing about the cause of his absence. And he still looked rocky.

Harry laid a hand on his shoulder. "Chuck says your car's blocking the drive, my boy. He can't get out."

With an effort Jim smiled. "It can't be my car. Thanks, Harry, I'll go see what the trouble is."

But it *was* his car. The low-slung Jaguar was parked in a very sloppy fashion, practically crosswise of the drive, right in the way of the other cars. He looked at it half-reproachfully, as if it had a life of its own and were responsible. Opening the door, he lowered himself into the driver's seat, started the engine, and swung the Jag back into the spot where it had been that afternoon: the parking strip by the walk that led to the back of the house. He had left it there when he got home from the station before dinner, and he knew he had not touched the wheel since.

He climbed out, raising an arm in a gesture of farewell as Chuck Bennett and his wife rolled past him in their convertible, and started back to the front door.

And then Chuck was backing the car at what looked like a highly reckless speed, and hitting the horn. He braked the car to a violent stop. "Jim!" he yelled. Simultaneously Peg flung open the door on her side, got out, and as Jim watched incredulously, ran into the house. He had never before seen a woman try to run like that in spike heels and a tight dress.

"What the—"

"Jim, get in. There's a dead woman in your drive."

He didn't question it. It was almost an answer; he had known that something was cock-eyed the minute he saw his car parked in that crazy position.

He didn't get in. The convertible top was down, but even so it would have taken too long to step over the side into the interior. He perched himself on the rear of the car, right behind Chuck.

"O.K."

They eased out the drive, the headlights tunneling into the dark ahead.

"Who is it?" Jim found the courage to ask.

"I don't know. Nobody I recognize."

And then, there it was: the dark body with its white face upwards, a white face dribbled with blood. The impossible position of the limbs told them that she was dead; a live human body would never look like that.

Jim slid to the ground and made his way around the car to stand over the form sprawled in the harsh illumination of the headlights.

He saw that it was Mrs. Wiebald.

Chapter 4

PEOPLE HAD been having breakfast in shifts all morning. Betty had yet to appear, and Marcia was keeping the coffee hot for her. She herself had eaten while standing at the stove; there had been no time to sit down.

She felt as if she had never closed her eyes all night. Perhaps she had, really, for half an hour once or twice, sandwiched in between the dark hours when she lay there staring at the ceiling, and the gray ones later when she watched the creeping light bring gradual shape and detail to all the objects in the bedroom, like developer acting on photographic paper.

By the time the police had gone there hadn't really been much left of the night. It must have been nearly midnight when the patrol car had arrived. Wooden-faced, the two officers had surveyed the scene and promptly sent for help. After that there were all the others—six or seven policemen in uniform, the police photographer, and Captain Fellini, looking official even in a business suit.

Captain Fellini had talked to them all in the living room, and one of the men in uniform had jotted down notes on what was said. It seemed to take hours.

Questions and answers from the interrogation had revolved all night in Marcia's head, repeatedly startling her into wakefulness just when she was about to drop off.

"You're sure the keys were in your car, Mr. Townsend?"

"Yes. I usually leave them there when I park in my own drive."

She hoped the police had believed that. Because thinking about it now she realized that it was very foolish indeed to leave the keys in the Jaguar so that anyone at all could take off with it. Yet it was true, Jim did generally leave the keys in it, here at home; in this kind of neighborhood one never gave much thought to the possibility of theft.

It was that which had put everyone at the party under suspicion—the fact that the keys were supposedly in the ignition. Anyone could have taken the Jaguar, as the captain pointed out, and struck down Mrs. Wiebald, accidentally or otherwise.

"If it was an accident, then why has no one come forward to say so?" Captain Fellini's bright, quick eyes had gone round the circle of guests, resting a moment on each one. "Is it because the person responsible is too well aware of the seriousness of a hit-and-run charge?" He paused, and then went on confidently, "I think we'll find the person who killed this woman. And I'd like to advise you all now, before it's too late, that pleading guilty to a charge of involuntary manslaughter is a lot easier to take than a conviction for murder."

Chuck Bennett had spoken up. "Why can't it have been kids coming in off the road, borrowing the car to take a joy ride?"

"A possibility, of course. Or it could have been some other person, not at this party, who knew that Mrs. Wiebald would be here and would be leaving early, when she got the children to bed. Someone with a grievance. We'll look into all that."

At last, fingerprinted and their names, addresses, and statements taken down, the guests had been allowed to leave and had filed soberly out to their cars to go home. To Marcia they seemed like a line of prisoners going on parole.

Finally, to her infinite relief, the police, too, had gone. Today, of course, they were back. She had watched them earlier from the front door and knew that they were measuring again out on the drive and searching the ground all around it. Just a few minutes ago one of them had appeared at the back door—a polite young man, and very nice-looking in his uniform— to ask if that was the door by which Mrs. Wiebald had left. She could see him now, examining the shrubbery out there and the ground beneath, searching, no doubt, for trace of someone who might have been waiting for Mrs. Wiebald to come out.

The door from the hall opened and Betty came into the kitchen. She was wearing a very chic housecoat.

"Hi. I must be the last one down."

"You are. I'm surprised you were lucky enough to sleep with the police out there beating the bushes."

"Oh, I wasn't asleep; I've just been lazing in bed. Any coffee, Marcia?"

"Anything you like."

"Just coffee, thanks. I never eat in the morning."

She took her cup over to the breakfast nook and sat with it, watching Marcia while she finished loading the dishwasher and wiping up the counters.

"I thought you had a maid to do all that."

"I wish I had. No, the maid last night was from the caterer's. You can't *get* help anymore; people feel they're too good to work for someone else in a menial capacity, I guess. Wait till you have a house and try to find just an ordinary cleaning girl. They're nonexistent."

Betty lifted a carefully outlined eyebrow. "That bad? Out in Chicago I hadn't any trouble getting help, just for the apartment . . ."

"Maybe you've got a knack, then; *some* people

around here have help of course, too. Karen does, certainly. Me, I still do the dusting and mop my own floors. At least this morning Jeannie—bless her heart—has taken the children off to the beach, which helps. A very good thing, too, having them out of the way while the police are crawling all over the place."

"Jeannie lives with you?"

"Ever since Jim's parents died. Jeannie was only fourteen then. Of course she was in boarding school, and later away at college, so we've only had her during vacations. To me, she's like the sister I never had. We're very close."

"Yes, I can imagine." As she spoke and tried to look pleasant, another wave of boredom washed over Betty. How was she going to stand the rest of this weekend, trapped with these dreadfully nice, dull people? At least, thank goodness, Mrs. Wiebald was no longer a cause for worry. And once again she thought with satisfaction of the swiftness with which the horrid old hag had been removed from the scene. It had been upsetting at the time, certainly, but this morning she could only feel tremendous relief at thought of the lucky "accident" which had erased so conveniently the ugly threat to her marriage and her whole present life.

In the living room Jim stood talking to Captain Fellini, who was this morning properly in uniform and doubly impressive. He had come out to see whether his men were turning up anything new. They weren't. Quint Rutledge, drinking one of the innumerable cups of coffee Marcia had served that morning, listened. He had dropped over, just on general principles, to find out how the investigation was getting on.

"So what we found, Mr. Townsend," the captain was saying, "was exactly what we expected to find. Your car, of course, was the instrument of death. And the only prints on the steering wheel were yours. They were the ones you made when you moved the car out of the way. Prior to that, quite obviously, the wheel had been wiped clean."

"Wiped *clean!*" Jim sent a startled glance toward Quint.

Fellini nodded. "No doubt about it. We can easily tell about a thing like that, you know: ordinarily the wheel would have been covered with fingerprints, palm prints—smudged and so on."

"Yes. I can see that." Jim stared grimly at the officer of the law. "The implications are pretty ugly, aren't they!"

"Well, it's not just a nice, simple accident. Whether she was run down on purpose we don't know yet, but we do know that whoever did it definitely has no intention of being connected with the woman's death."

Jim nodded and turned away to gaze glumly out the windows at the array of police cars in the turning circle.

"What about outsiders, people other than the ones here at the party?" asked Quint.

"Well, if it was kids 'borrowing' the car they left no trace. As to enemies Mrs. Wiebald may have had—we'll find out. I've got men on the job talking to everyone who knew her."

"Has the time of death been established?"

"Probably between eight and nine, according to the Medical Examiner—which checks with the time Mrs. Townsend said she paid her and Mrs. Wiebald left. She'd been dead perhaps three hours by the time we got here."

Involuntarily Jim sucked in his breath. It was horrible to think of her lying there undiscovered hour after hour while inside the party was still going on.

The captain turned to go. In the foyer he hesitated. "Mr. Townsend, do you actually *remember* leaving your keys in the car yesterday? Or do you just think you might have?" His dark eyes under the graying hair were extraordinarily keen.

Jim shrugged. "I don't honestly remember. But it's a habit of mine."

"A convenient one, under the circumstances. For you, that is. It certainly widens the field." Whether or not Fellini was being sarcastic Jim did not know.

The captain went on out into the sunshine, talked for a few minutes to the sergeant in charge of combing the area, and then drove away. Jim watched him from

59

the front steps and when he had gone returned to Quint in the living room. With a grunt he slumped into a chair.

Quint lit a cigarette and squinted as the smoke curled up. "Obviously anyone could have taken your car. What interests me, Jim, is how the woman happened to be killed. Was it an accident, and the person who had borrowed the car then tried in a panic to remove all evidence of his presence? Or did someone kill Mrs. Wiebald deliberately? It seems an odd way to murder anyone—the attempt could so easily have missed if she got off the drive in time. But then it could have been the only means at hand. What kind of person was she?"

"Oh, you heard her described—when they asked us all those questions last night. Middle-aged widow, fifty-five or so, I'd say. She was a very friendly, talkative sort —talked constantly, in fact."

"Inquisitive, would you say—prying?"

"No, she didn't pry. She was just interested. She was devoted to all her clients; she baby-sat all the time, you know. And she looked on everyone she sat for as family, practically."

"Ah." Quint blew out a cloud of smoke and watched it thoughtfully. "Do you think she could have been blackmailing any of them?"

"Oh, no." Jim's response was quick, sure. "She wasn't that sort. She *liked* the people she worked for, as I say."

"Still, she could have come into possession of damaging information of some sort. Working in homes, taking such an interest—almost like a relative as you describe her—she must have known a great deal about some of her employers. She could easily have been in a position to do someone harm—she could have threatened to interfere, on the basis of some private knowledge. Blackmail needn't have come into it. She just may have had the goods on someone, and whoever it was had to stop her before she took action of some kind."

Jim looked upset. "Do you really think so? Has it got to be a murder? I still think some kind of accident—"

Quint sat relaxed, sure in his own mind. He lifted an eyebrow quizzically at Jim. "And how do you explain the fact that they took your car to have the 'accident' with?"

"Well, it could have been kids; the captain's saying there's no trace of any doesn't prove a thing. They wouldn't have left calling cards in any case."

"And when they hit Mrs. Wiebald they'd have kept on going and ditched the car elsewhere. They'd have been too scared to bring it *back* up the drive and then have to escape on foot."

Jim looked taken aback. "Yes." After a moment's thought he nodded. "I suppose you're right."

"And I can see no reason why any of your guests would have borrowed your car. Any harmless reason, that is. No one that was here last night would have thought of borrowing your Jag without asking you first. True?"

"True." Jim had turned the color of putty. "There's one possibility, Quint, that you haven't mentioned. I'm only too well aware of it myself."

"What's that?" Quint glanced narrowly at the big man opposite him, attentive to the unexpected thickening in Jim's voice.

"*I* could have done it myself."

"But you were passed out in the den. You weren't even operating at the time."

"That's just it. I could have been. You know I have these blackouts when I've had too much to drink; there can be long periods of an evening that are a complete blank in my mind. And about last night: I can't remember a thing that happened from sometime before dinner was served till Harry came up to me and said I'd have to go move my car."

"Harry asked you to move it? I thought it was Chuck who wanted to leave just then."

"It was Chuck's car mine was blocking—yes. But it was Harry who came into the house and told me so."

Quint gazed off in thought.

Jim's voice grated harshly. "So you see, I could very well have run her down and not remember a thing about it."

Quint glanced quickly at Jim, his eyelids contracting in their characteristic squint, a sort of nervous tic.

"Now, wait a minute, Jim! I never want to hear you say anything like *that* again. Not to the police, not to your friends, not to anyone!"

"But it's the truth." The agony of self-doubt was all too evident in his face. "I mean, it *could* be the truth."

"*No!*" Quint leaned forward in his chair, his arms crossed on his knees, and looked Jim intently in the eye. Then the corner of his mouth quirked up. "Your conscience is bothering you over your passing out last night, that's all. Any head-shrinker would tell you so. But you're overdoing it by a mile. Confess to a murder? I never took you for a hair-shirt fancier."

"I'm not. But do you have any idea what it's like not to remember anything about the night before? It's happened to me more times than I'd care to count. Only before, it never mattered particularly. Now with this—"

"Forget it. You were asleep in the den. How could you have gotten in your car and—"

"But I wasn't asleep. Not then. Jeannie told me she brought me a cup of coffee just after Mrs. Wiebald went out the back door. She waked me up and I said something to her, so I was conscious. But I don't remember a thing about it."

"Well if you were with Jeannie—"

"She gave me the coffee and left. So I don't know where I was or what I was doing."

"You probably went right back to sleep." He smiled.

"Besides, Jim, you're not going to tell me that if you *did* go out there and somehow accidentally run over your sitter you would then deliberately do a thing like wiping your prints off the wheel? The act of a calculating criminal? You're not capable of it."

"Sober, no." His big, honest face was haunted. "But drunks are crafty—you know that, Quint. Faced with having killed someone . . . how do I know *what* I might have done? And I wouldn't," he added heavily, "remember it now."

Betty came out of the shower to find Tom lounging in the easy chair by the window of the guest room. She slipped off her robe and started getting dressed.

"Can't we get out of here, Tom?" I'm fed to the teeth with these people."

He looked up at her in surprise. "I thought you were having a good time. Last night at the party—"

"Oh, anyone can act gay at a party. A couple of drinks and you don't care who you're talking to. Actually, it wasn't too bad, either. But it'll be the same crowd, I'm sure, at the Judges' party this evening, and they don't wear all *that* well. And Jim and Marcia—my God, they're so domestic it sets my teeth on edge. I don't doubt they're a complete fake—he's probably sleeping with his secretary, and she's too dumb to know it."

Tom frowned. "Marcia's not dumb. And Jim's not

64

sleeping around, either. Where do you get these ideas? They're probably the happiest couple I know."

"Then heaven deliver me from such connubial bliss! Is that really what you want me to turn into, another Marcia? She is *too* dumb: she even admitted to me she can't get any help—does all her own housework. Any time I'd scrub the floors with all that money coming in! Well, even in Chicago with a small apartment, I managed to get someone. But the point is, they're dull as dishwater, both of them. I don't see how you can stand them."

Tom's face quivered as he tried to keep down his displeasure. "I don't think you've given them a fair chance, Betty. When you're better acquainted I'm sure you'll find that they're very agreeable people. And if you don't like them, please don't criticize them in front of me; I'm extremely fond of them."

She was silent while she wriggled into her dress. "You mean then that you prefer your friends to me." There was acid in her voice.

"I said nothing of the kind." Once again, he thought, she was putting words into his mouth, twisting what he said.

"Anyway, I take it you intend to stay the weekend, even if I'm miserable."

"Of *course* I'm going to stay the weekend, and so are you. Surely you haven't forgotten that we're in the midst of a police investigation? The captain distinctly said last night that none of us was to leave town until he gave the all clear."

"Well he could undoubtedly make an exception if you asked him to; it's not as if we were criminals."

"I have no intention of asking him. You must know, certainly, that I wouldn't consider leaving. Jim and Marcia need us for moral support."

"Oh, I see." Her features, molded now by anger, were ugly. "*Dear* Jim and Marcia. And dear Jeannie. I'm sure *she* wants us to stay."

"I have no idea."

"Well, if you don't, I do. I hope you were properly amused at her performance last night."

"What 'performance'? What are you talking about?"

"Jeannie throwing herself at you. All evening. Making with those big baby-blue eyes of hers."

"You're out of your mind. We're old friends, that's all, and she wasn't throwing herself at me. I was as interested in talking to her as she was in talking to me—"

"Oh, you *were?*" Betty widened her brown eyes at him.

"I didn't mean it *that* way." His voice was hard. "You're trying to make something out of nothing. Jeannie was just a kid when I knew her, and as far as I'm concerned, she's still a kid. I taught her to sail, and that's what we were talking about mostly last night: boats. That's all, just boats."

"Well, you needn't bite my head off, just because I mentioned your precious Jeannie."

She had finished dressing now and was putting on her jewelry—a heavy charm bracelet and the big diamond that was her engagement ring.

"Oh, by the way. My diamond watch is missing."

"Missing?" Tom looked over at her. "You wore it to the party last night, I saw it on your wrist."

"Yes. But the catch seemed to be loose so I took it off during the evening and put it here in its case. It's gone. I've been through the drawers and my suitcase this morning and it's not here. Someone must have stolen it."

Tom sighed deeply.

Jeannie lay on her stomach on the narrow crescent of sand. It was a small beach and stony, with just this little strip where the children could wade out without hurting their feet on the rocks. Her chin resting on her folded arms, she watched Tim, aged six, and Suzie, aged four, as they played at the edge of the water. Here on the Sound there was no surf to worry about.

Except for the nightmare period after her parents' sudden death in the automobile crash, she couldn't remember a day when she had awakened with such a weight of dread upon her. If it were not for the actual events of last night she might have thought that her black mood of the evening had induced in her a despair of everything, darkening the aspect of all the world about her in accordance with her own feelings. But this was not the case. Poor Mrs. Wiebald was indisputably dead, and dead in a violent manner evocative of horror in all those even remotely connected with her. Worse than this, almost—for nothing could now be done for Mrs. Wiebald except to bury her—Jim felt responsible. She knew he did. It had happened at his house, as a result of her being employed by him, and most fiendish of all, it had been done with his car.

Jim had alarmed her, the way he talked, the way he kept asking her about the cup of coffee she had brought him. She couldn't miss the fact that he was trying to account to himself for his own movements. Surely he couldn't have any idea that he could himself have taken the car while he was blacked out and . . . But she had a horrible feeling that he did think just that. She remembered what Tom had said last night: how his fraternity brothers used to kid Jim about what he had done during his memory lapses. To her brother it would be credible that he could have done it.

And added to the tragedy of Mrs. Wiebald, her brother's worries, and her own helpless attachment to Tom was her feeling about Betty Graham. Betty was all wrong for Tom. She was sure of it. She was also sure that it was not jealousy or sour grapes on her part that convinced her of it. Betty was a terrible person. It was there in her face—a greedy face, a vain face, a lying face.

But Tom loved her. So what was there to hope for? That Betty would prove the wrong wife, that she would make Tom unhappy? No, she couldn't wish that. But for Tom's future she felt a dread. It was a double ache —one for him, and one for herself. She couldn't help wishing that Tom had come back a year ago instead of now: he would still have been free. Would he have cared for her? She would never know.

But one thing she did know. She couldn't possibly wish that he had not come back at all. She would rather be suffering as she was now, helpless in the clutch of an emotion so painful she had never felt anything to compare with it, than to consider a world without Tom. She had known as soon as she woke up in the morning that yesterday's renewal of an old love, devastating now in its mature form, had been no momentary thing; it was here to stay.

"A letter for you." Jeannie handed it to Betty as she stood there in the big, elegantly-papered foyer in her bathing suit leafing through the mail. She had picked it up at the box as she pulled into the drive just now bringing the children home from the beach for lunch.

"For me?" Betty couldn't have been more surprised.

"I expect you're swamped with invitations now that

you and Tom are back East. Following you around on weekends, even!"

"Yes, I expect it's something of the sort." But she sounded doubtful. In fact Jeannie thought she looked downright uneasy as she took the letter and returned up the stairs down which she had just come.

Betty didn't open it until she was safe in their room, alone. Tom had gone off somewhere, she didn't know where or even care at the moment.

She stared at the envelope. It was obviously not an invitation. It was a plain white business envelope, no return address, and her name and the address were printed in an odd sort of backhand. There was no postmark. The stamp had a black mark over it, more like an ink smudge than a cancellation.

No one would write to her here, she knew that: the only people who even had knowledge of her whereabouts were the ones who had been invited to the party last night. As she looked at the envelope her heart pounded. Whatever this was, it wasn't going to be something nice.

With the care that was second nature to her now, she locked the door. Then with a nail file from the dresser she slashed open the missive.

Inside was a newspaper clipping, faintly yellowed already, although it was only three years old. It was the picture of her that had appeared in the papers along with others of persons killed in the train wreck. "Mrs.

Albert Treadly Melinder, one of the dead" read the caption.

She stared at it, stunned. Her vision blurred, then cleared. Surely this was a dream, a nightmare; in a minute she would wake up.

She sank down on one of the twin beds, her mind empty of all thought, aware only of the feel of the textured spread beneath the fingers of one hand, in the other the crumpled edge of envelope. Outside a bird sang, happily, annoyingly; and feeling a little sick, she watched the leaves of the big oak tree just outside the window as they swayed with a breath of warm breeze. It was not a dream.

The clipping lay on her lap. Automatically she checked the envelope to see if there was anything more.

There was. Inside the flap, written in the same odd backhand, was a message.

"*Need I say more?*" That was what it said. That was all.

Now, swiftly, her anger formed.

How dare they! And who was it? Was this a threat?

The anger cleared her mind and sent it darting first one way, then another, in rage, seeking an answer.

What *was* this? Blackmail? Or merely cruel sport, at her expense? Was she to be left quivering in fear of exposure, helpless, never knowing at what moment her mask would be ripped away?

71

She found no answers and went on to a more useful question.

Why? That was the important thing. She became calmer, concentrated all her attention on the question. Yes, she knew this was the right approach. Why? The person who sent her this must have had some reason. Something to gain from terrorizing her? Personal satisfaction of some kind? Vengeance?

The letter had not been mailed. That was clearly an ink spot on the stamp, put there to suggest that it had gone through the post office. It had, then, been placed by hand in the mailbox with the other letters.

Mrs. Wiebald had not lived long enough to place any kind of threat in the box: the mailbox was one of those rural ones on a post by the road—she knew because she had noticed the name on it as they arrived yesterday. So Mrs. Wiebald could not possibly have been the one: she had died halfway out the drive.

With a quick, cunning leap, her mind recognized the tormentor. But she forestalled confirmation at the edge of her consciousness while she slowly eliminated every other possibility. Thoroughly she went over all the people she had met last night, discarding them one by one. She paused at Quint Rutledge. He had not liked her, that she knew. But he had no means of knowing who she really was, and furthermore she felt instinctively that he was too subtle to do anything so crude, so concrete, as to put a newspaper clipping in an envelope and send it to her. He would consider anything of the sort childish and a waste of time.

Harry Judge? He had made that opening gambit of "Haven't we met?" But that had been just a line. If he had actually recognized her, she would have known it. Besides, this threat couldn't be from Harry, it wasn't in character. He had clearly been quite smitten with her; he would do nothing which could cause her to pack her bags and flee back to the city just when he was getting his campaign well under way.

Marcia or Jim were patently out. They were sweet and kind, if horribly dull, and had made it clear that they would do everything they could for Tom's bride.

The rest of the party could be eliminated with ease.

Except Jeannie. Of course. Jeannie was the one she had been saving to consider last, because several lines of reasoning converged on Tom's little protégé in a quite convincing pattern.

To begin with, it was she who had handed her the letter. And all that covering jazz about its looking like an invitation! Anyone could see with half a glance that it was not.

As to evidence, Jeannie was the most likely candidate. It was she to whom Mrs. Wiebald had been talking in the kitchen last night; the gabby old piece could have passed on quite a bit of information before she clammed up in front of Betty and walked out. She could have given Jeannie her name and everything. In fact Jeannie was probably the only one to whom she had had the chance to say anything.

And motive for this sneaky, threatening attack? Jeannie had that, too. She was in love with Tom; that was as plain as could be. Betty had watched her when the girl hadn't known she was looking; she had practically devoured Tom alive, just looking at him. Those great big blue eyes were unable, in their stupid innocence, to dissemble.

Yes, Jeannie would have been just the one to make use of the information about Liz Melinder when it fell into her hands: a way to get back at the girl who had married the man she was crazy about.

Betty went over it all again: she wouldn't want to make a mistake. She intended dealing with Jeannie in some way. She wasn't going to let her get away with this scare technique. One question, of course, was where Jeannie could have gotten hold of the clipping so fast? But there was probably an easy answer. Some friend of the Townsends, perhaps, had died in the train wreck. The clipping could easily have been saved all this time, and Jim's sister would have known just where to lay her hands on it.

Having identified her adversary, Betty turned next to an assessment of Jeannie's probable intentions. Was she just being spiteful, trying to make Betty squirm, or was she going to do something about her discovery? It was clear that if what Jeannie wanted was Tom—and that much was settled in Betty's mind—she would have to do something more. She couldn't suppose Betty would clear out, leaving everything she had worked so hard for, just because of a simple threat. She wouldn't tell Tom—that would be much too bald an action and would damage her own prospects with him. Jeannie was smart, she would think of something better than that. Such as a call to Al Melinder. "Do you know that your wife is a weekend guest at a house in Rockton? Why, yes, indeed. Go see for yourself. No, she isn't dead at all. And she's a blonde now. Yes. And just say a friend told you. I'm the friend. You don't need my name, just your wife's name—her new name."

Something like that. Tom would never know Jeannie had had a thing to do with it. Oh, yes, that would work nicely!

Well, she would have to stop her. Stop her for sure.

Marcia was making sandwiches for lunch when Tom wandered into the kitchen. The children had been served theirs already; through the window over the sink he could see them eating at a miniature picnic table under the trees in the back yard.

He dropped onto the yellow step stool and watched her.

"What's the matter?" she asked. "I thought Jim was

low enough today, but you look almost as bad. We don't need two of you like that."

"Oh, I don't know."

"Maybe it's just the general atmosphere today. Even Jeannie seems depressed—like a zombie. And she's usually the most cheerful of the lot. I suppose the accident has sort of cast a pall on things. Poor Mrs. Wiebald! I still can't understand what in the world could have happened. Jim won't even talk about it. He discussed it with Quint, I guess, when he was here this morning, but I don't know what they said. Has Jim said anything to you about what he thinks might have happened?"

"No. All I can get out of him is monosyllables."

"It was very queer, wasn't it. How she was killed." Frowning, she cut the sandwiches into triangles and began to arrange them on a platter. Tom helped.

"I expect the police will get to the bottom of it—eventually. I wouldn't worry."

Marcia looked up at him searchingly and he saw the worry deep in her eyes. "Will they?" She turned away.

He changed the subject, though hardly to a more cheerful topic.

"Did Betty tell you she can't find her diamond watch?"

"Her watch?" She turned quickly to face him. "That gorgeous thing? I was admiring it last night. Why, what in the world—"

"She seems convinced it was stolen." Tom felt embarrassed as he said it.

"Stolen! Couldn't she have lost it? It might have slipped off her wrist somehow. When did she see it last?"

"Last night. She said the catch was loose and she took it off during the party and put it in its case upstairs. It's not there."

Marcia shook her head slowly. "There was no one here last night who could have taken it. No kleptomaniacs among the guests, and Mrs. Wiebald was as honest as could be—she's been sitting for everyone we know for ages, and never a thing taken; that kind of news would get around, you know—anything disappearing from the houses where she sat. Now the maid who was serving I don't know too well—she's from the caterer's. But there again, working for an outfit like that—they wouldn't employ her if she was light fingered, with all the mink stoles lying about at parties. Besides, I'm sure she was never upstairs; no reason to be."

"You think Betty must have mislaid it?"

"I don't know *what* to think!" Indeed she didn't. Only one thought did come into her head, from whence she didn't know: all of a sudden they had not only a violent death but a theft, and that within twenty-four hours after Betty Graham had come into the house. Marcia reproached herself sharply for entertaining

77

even momentarily any such idea. Whatever she was, Betty was certainly not a murderer; and there was no reason to suppose she was a liar either.

"I'll tell everyone in the house it's missing," she said. "And surely it'll turn up somehow."

"I don't know why women want things like diamond watches anyway; if they have one they say it's too good to wear and leave it in a drawer and worry about its being stolen while they're out."

"Well, I don't have one, so I wouldn't know. There are too many other things I'd rather have, I guess." She smiled.

"You're a no-nonsense girl, Marcia—you always were."

"*That* doesn't even sound like a compliment, darn it!"

"Oh, but it is. I've always thought Jim was a very lucky guy."

"Well, thank you. But you're married yourself, now. No cause for envy."

Tom sighed. "I don't know. I frequently get to feeling I just wasn't cut out for matrimony. I don't think Betty's got much of a prize in me."

Marcia was shocked. "*You*, Tom? Any girl with you for a husband should count herself blessed!"

"Well, you haven't tried living with me, so—"

"Propositioning you, is he dear?" Jim came in from

the dining room. "Maybe you should give it a whirl. As of today, I'm much too old for you: I feel a thousand."

"Hangover this morning, old boy?" asked Tom.

"Miraculously, no. Last night I sobered up totally in about five seconds, and it was as if I'd never had a drink. No, it's just events and no sleep and probably the fifteen or so cups of coffee that have got me now."

At lunch Marcia announced that Betty's beautiful watch was missing. "Unless it's turned up somehow?" she asked Betty.

"No. I'm afraid it isn't going to just 'turn up'."

"In other words, you think it was stolen."

"Well, yes."

"We can check with the police and see if it was among Mrs. Wiebald's things," Marcia suggested. "Jim can go out right now and ask one of the officers who's still here."

"Oh, no." Betty was quick to oppose the idea. "I wouldn't want to register a complaint, not with the woman dead, you know. It wouldn't seem right."

Tom looked up in apparent surprise. Perhaps he had not expected his wife to be so considerate of someone else's feelings—especially those of a dead woman who presumably no longer had any.

"I doubt very much," said Jim, "that she took it. But it clearly won't bother her any if we ask. Won't bother the police, either."

"Thanks," Tom put in. "I think Betty would rather you didn't."

"Actually," Jim added, "if the police found it in Mrs. Wiebald's possession the fact will come out eventually: they'll be asking us about it. After all, a child of five would know that a diamond watch like that one is out of financial reach for an ordinary sitter like Mrs. Wiebald."

And there the matter was dropped.

It was mid-afternoon before Betty had the chance she wanted to speak to Jeannie alone. Looking out the guest room window, she observed Jim's sister in the parking strip, batting tennis balls against the closed garage doors. She went down. The police, she noticed, seemed to have gone.

"You're good at that."

Jeannie stopped. "I'm trying to keep in form. I'm giving tennis lessons along with sailing at the day camp. Got to keep ahead of the kids a little." She looked lovely in the crisp white tennis outfit, with its trim shorts and immaculate top.

"I wanted to talk to you."

"What about?" Jeannie swung the racket idly back and forth at her side.

"I think you know what about."

Jeannie glanced up, puzzled. "I'm sorry. Maybe I've missed something, but I don't know just what—"

Betty's lips twitched in annoyance. "The letter, of course. That letter you handed me this morning."

"What about it?" The racket hung motionless now in the slim, brown hand.

"It was you who sent it. I know that."

The natural light brows contracted in a quick frown. "I don't know what you're talking about. I handed you a letter—yes. It was in the mail with the others."

"Don't give me that." Rage crept into Betty's voice, edged with frustration. "You sent it."

"But I didn't." The beginnings of anger sparked in Jeannie's straight gaze. Clearly, she was prepared to stand her ground in face of attack.

"You're trying to frighten me," said Betty slowly. "Well, it won't work." The big, luminous eyes narrowed to two vicious slits. "You know what happened to Mrs. Wiebald. Well, it could happen to you. Don't kid yourself. Just remember—you don't push me out."

Jeannie frowned and studied her, not frightened by her words, but puzzled. "Betty, I don't know what you're talking about. Whatever you just said, I wish you hadn't. It doesn't make any sense to me. You've no reason to threaten me, though that's what it sounded like. I wouldn't harm a hair of your head, as you should know; Tom's too dear a friend to us all here for any of us to wish you harm. If you're receiving threatening letters, well then I think you ought to tell Tom and let him deal with it."

Betty's gaze stayed on her, frozen. Was it possible that she had made a mistake? The girl's manner had the stamp of truth. Perhaps she had not been the one to send her the clipping. In that case she had made a grave error: she had informed Jeannie that something was wrong, terribly wrong; one didn't receive threatening letters such as she had implied she'd received, just out of a clear blue sky.

"Perhaps I was mistaken," she said. "I expect it was some kind of a joke, then—one of my friends must have sent it to me thinking to give me a good laugh." Her lips quirked up in a smile, but not a very convincing one. "Since you handed me the letter—I'm sorry, I thought—"

"That's all right. I'll forget it if you like." Jeannie regarded her quizzically. "We'll just say it was a mistake."

"O.K. Apparently it *was* a mistake."

Jeannie looked at her a long moment. She felt she must say something more.

"Betty, I don't know what's back of the letter business. It sounds pretty ugly. Is it a poison pen letter, something of that kind? Or a threat? It must be something like that from the way you spoke of it. You needn't tell me if you don't want to. But it sounds—serious. I want you to know that none of us in this house would write such a letter, or could possibly have any reason to. We're your friends, Tom's friends. If I can help, I'll be glad to. Can I?"

"No." An ugly, mottled flush had spread over Betty's face. "I told you, I'm sure it was a joke of some kind— and not a very funny one."

"Then you really should tell Tom. Let him deal with it."

"I'm not worried about it now."

"But you were when you thought I wrote it. Why?"

Betty was silent for a minute, and when she finally answered it was with a clear coating of dislike on her voice. "Because of Tom. You'd like to get him for yourself." With gratification Betty noted the quick, startled movement, like that of a person believing himself alone, who suddenly discovers he is being watched. Jeannie had thought no one knew? The wide eyes gazed at her, stricken. "You can't deny it, can you!"

"I *can* deny it!" The voice was a little husky. "I'd never in this world make a play for a married man. That sort of thing's not in my personal book of rules."

"Rules aren't always the deciding factor; in fact they're frequently the first things to go overboard— aren't they! And I noticed you don't deny that you have eyes for Tom. Well, he's married to *me* and don't forget it! Quit looking his way or I'll see that you're very sorry."

Jeannie bridled. "Look, I'm not used to having peo-

83

ple threaten me; and that doesn't mean I'm going to *become* used to it, either. I don't know what kind of world you come from, Betty, but it sounds as though you had better leave it well behind you—and fast. Things aren't like that in Tom's world, and it's time you found out that they're not."

"The genteel upper crust?"

"Nothing to do with upper crust, or middle—whatever—"

It was just then that Suzie came up the drive towards them from the road, her shorts sagging dangerously with the weight of treasures in the pockets; Suzie was a rock collector. Her little red tennis shoes, one untied and the other with the lace hopelessly knotted, carried her eagerly forward.

"Aunt Jeannie, guess what I found. Look!" She held it out. "Real diamonds!" Real rhinestones would have been equally real diamonds to Suzie. "It's a watch. It even runs."

Jeannie knelt down by her. "Oh, that's wonderful, Suzie! It's Mrs. Graham's watch; she lost it yesterday." She took it in her hand. "Where did you find it, honey?"

The child pointed. "Over by my house." Jeannie's eyes followed in the direction indicated by the stubby finger.

"Suzie means her playhouse; it's a secret place of hers

under the bushes." She nodded, frowning lightly, towards a clump of ornamental shrubs out near the front of the drive; the place was quite near the spot where Mrs. Wiebald had met her end. "Run and show us, dear, exactly where it was."

Obediently Suzie hurried back to the scene of her find, not waiting for the slower adults to follow.

"I can't understand how it could have gotten out *there*." Jeannie still held the watch. Absently she snapped the catch and then unfastened it again. She hadn't meant to—the motion had been automatic. The catch, she noticed, didn't seem to be loose at all.

"*I* can." Betty's words were cold, crisp. "She stole it. The sitter. She must have been holding it when the car hit her and it flew out of her hand." She reached out to Jeannie for the watch, her palm open, demanding.

"Oh, I'm sorry!" Hastily Jeannie passed it to her. "I didn't mean to hang onto it." They were following Suzie out the drive, now. "But I just can't agree that Mrs. Wiebald stole it. Something different from that must have happened."

"Such as?" Betty eyed her narrowly.

"I really can't imagine."

Could she possibly suspect, Betty wondered, that Mrs. Wiebald had been offered the watch in payment for silence? She remembered how the woman had stood there in the darkness of the drive, turning the watch

85

this way and that, trying to catch the glint of the diamonds in the distant house lights, trying to make up her mind.

They had almost reached the spot where Mrs. Wiebald had been struck down. Key points had been marked by the police on the blacktop, which resembled now some sinister game to be played by giants. At the center of the game was the tracing of a human form, spread-eagled. Without comment the two girls abandoned the pavement in favor of the grass.

Suzie had reached her goal and stood by the weeping shrub that cascaded down to the ground in a green curtain half concealing a dust-floored hiding place.

"Right here, Aunt Jeannie. It was right here." She pulled the branches back to show exactly where. Not in the secret house, where the police, Jeannie was thinking, would no doubt have looked, but under the trailing ends of the branches where they lay on the grass.

"My goodness, Suzie," said her aunt, "I'm surprised you saw it at all."

"I didn't, nearly. I was coming out the back door. This is the back door. And it was just on the ground." She grinned up expectantly at Betty.

Betty had put the watch back on. "Well, thanks," she said without warmth. "I'm lucky you found it."

With Jeannie she started back to the house. Suzie lingered behind where she had spotted a cluster of nice pink stones for her collection.

"Yes, you *are* lucky. The police went over every inch of ground out here this morning without turning it up; it was probably in the only spot they missed."

Once again they walked on the grass, avoiding the drive.

"Guess I'd better go and tell Tom I've got it back." Betty had had more than enough of Jeannie, and further discussion of events might at any moment take some awkward turning. As they approached the house she swung off and headed for the front door.

Jeannie reclaimed her tennis racket from the grass at the edge of the parking strip, where she had laid it down when Suzie came up with the watch. She stayed on in the shade by the garage, whacking the balls savagely against the wood, her mind free to roam over the facts that seemed to have come to light. Well, not facts. Intimations. She didn't like the smell of the whole thing. And she hoped indeed that her feelings for Tom weren't prejudicing her against his wife.

But no matter how she looked at it, something was seriously amiss. Someone had sent a threatening letter to Betty. Of that much she was sure. And unless she was stark, staring mad, Betty, thinking *she* had sent it, had threatened to kill her. Unbelievable as that seemed, there was no blinking the fact that Mrs. Wiebald had been killed yesterday, quite possibly murdered. And Mrs. Wiebald, it might just seem, had thought it strange that Betty looked like someone else she used to know.

Who? Well, now they would never know. Mrs. Wiebald was dead. Had her knowledge been damaging enough to make her death a necessity? And Betty's missing watch had turned up at the scene of the death. Nor was the catch loose, as Betty had declared. Oh, hell! She missed the ball and decided to quit. By now she practically had Tom's wife a murderer!

Jeannie felt sick. What a diseased imagination she must have, and a sick soul, she decided, as she slipped on the racket cover and tightened the screws on the press, to let her feeling for Tom lead her so far astray! Wishful thinking, and wicked wishful thinking it was. Tom was not for her and never would be.

I'll go wash my hair under the shower, she thought. Maybe the cool water running over her brain would bring back her good sense. If anything would.

It wasn't any one thing. It was everything, Tom thought. Every single thing seemed to be wrong today. He was a fine one to try to cheer Jim up—he'd talked to him ever since lunch and didn't seem to have made a dent in the gloom in which Jim had encased himself. The guy seemed convinced that he'd killed the woman last night without knowing it. He'd sat there in the den, glassy eyed, seeing it happen in his mind's eye, over and over again. By the time Tom had gotten up and left, his friend hadn't seemed any better, just more confirmed in this fixed opinion.

And what in the world had gotten into Betty? She'd actually been packing her suitcase when he went up to the room looking for her just now. He'd put a stop to that, of course, and he interpreted this sudden frenzy to leave as just another incidence of the hysteria that seemed to have gripped her periodically since they had come East. Though why she should be so upset out here, away from New York City and all its old memories he could not understand. She had seemed almost desperate when for the second time today he had told her they couldn't possibly leave; she had stared at him as if he were persecuting her. Why was she so set on getting away from here? Because she was bored? That was absurd. The people here were not that uniformly dull. They were good friends of his and she should try to take more of an interest. Finally she had said she didn't feel well, but nothing very definite. Again she had said maybe she was pregnant. Then there was even less reason to go tearing off in the car, as he had pointed out to her; she should just lie down till she felt better. She had finally agreed.

But what was back of all this?

Taking a cigarette from the pack in his pocket, he lit it thoughtfully as he stared out the big, open front door. He wandered out onto the steps and turned up the drive. It would do him good to take a walk, get some air, get away from things.

As he came to the end of the house, the garage end

where the parking strip jutted off to the side of the blacktop drive, he caught sight of Jeannie, head down, coming around the corner of the garage, a tennis racket in her hand.

"Hi." He stopped.

"Oh!" She was startled. "Hello, Tom."

"Been playing tennis, I see."

"Oh, just practicing against the garage doors."

Something unfolded within his chest and he felt better than he had all day. "Is there someplace we could play?"

She hesitated. "Why, yes. Duncans, just down the road, have a court. We're welcome to use it any time."

"Got an extra racket?"

"Of course. You really want to play?"

"It seems like the first good idea I've had today."

They collected another racket from the garage and walked out the drive to the road. Mrs. Wiebald's battered old car was still parked on the grass by the mailbox; no one had come to take it away. Jeannie turned to the left and Tom swung along beside her, the two of them keeping on the black asphalt edge of the road next to the weedy verge. The houses were not close together here; each nestled snugly in the middle of a three or four acre tract of trees and grass. Two or three houses down the road they turned into a faint path through some shrubbery and came out by a well-maintained clay court, its backstop fencing covered with climbing roses, most of the blooms past their prime, like faded ball-room decorations.

"You definitely have the advantage," said Tom, taking the cover from the borrowed racket and giving it a trial swing. It felt good in his hand. "I haven't been on a tennis court in at least three years."

Jeannie smiled, and again Tom had that odd sinking feeling that he seemed to get when he looked at her. "Well," she said, "you're bigger than I am, with a longer reach. It'll even out."

Tom was quite rusty, but as they played he improved a little, and soon they had a good game going. They both laughed at the ones he missed, and then he made up for them with his fast serve, which was hard to return. He won the set.

"Let's play another, shall we?" asked Tom. He hadn't felt so at ease, so unharried, in weeks. The pong of the ball against the rackets had a restorative sound. And there was something about Jeannie—he liked watching her as she swung on the ball, as she smiled at him across the net, friendly, not talking much, just there.

Tom didn't do so well in the second set. Jeannie even had a feeling he was fumbling on purpose, letting her win. Towards the end of it he remarked, "It's obviously going to have to be best two out of three, isn't it?"

"It looks like it."

The third set went slowly. Neither of them was in a hurry. Several times they paused and exchanged a few remarks before the serve. It was Tom who won at last.

"Thanks," he said as they stood together at the end of the net. As he looked down at her he had an almost uncontrollable desire to take her in his arms and just hold her, to feel her cheek against his. It was impossible. What could he be thinking of?

They walked back up the road.

"You're going to the Judges' dinner tonight?" he asked.

"I was, but not now. Since Mrs. Wiebald was killed —she was to stay with the children, you know—well, I don't know who else Marcia could have gotten, but I thought it would be less upsetting for Tim and Suzie if I sat with them. They were very fond of Mrs. Wiebald, and Marcia told them what happened to her; she had to—part of it at least—because they would have found out somehow, you know."

"Oh." Tom felt unreasonably disappointed. "Then you're baby-sitting. I'm sorry. I wish you were going."

As they walked up the drive towards the Townsends' big, white house, its walls shaded by oaks and maples from the afternoon sun beating down hard upon the black slate roof, Tom became aware of a deep reluctance to go in, to face Betty again in a continuation of the scene she had staged before. Not just yet. For a little while he would like to prolong the hiatus.

He eyed his car, parked in the circle of the turn-around in front of the house, the circle that had been wholly blocked last night by Jim's car parked slantingly across it, bottling up the transport for the whole dinner party and necessitating Jim's coming out and putting his fingerprints on the steering wheel. Odd, that—very odd.

"How about a drive—just around?" he asked Jeannie. For a moment he thought she was going to accept, but then she shook her head.

"Thanks, I've got things to do. Why don't you take Betty?"

But he didn't take Betty. What he really wanted was to get off to himself, to sort things out. Jeannie would have been no deterrent to that, and her presence beside him would have added something he needed—a sense of harmony, of belonging with other people.

Strange, he thought as he swung the car around the circle, that feeling of kinship he had with Jeannie. He eased the car past her with a sharp sense of something missed, and he smiled at her standing there on the front steps, her chin resting on the top of her tennis racket.

He headed towards the shore, someplace where he could park the car and look out over the water. That always brought him peace.

Until he reached it he didn't even try to think, but drove along, his mind a blessed blank. He knew the shore here, and so he headed for a high spot above the beach, where he wouldn't tangle with bathers or fishermen. It was a sort of miniature cliff located at the end of a grassy lane wandering away from the shore road, on a piece of land that lay between two large estates. He climbed out of the car and sat on the long, tough grass, looking down at the strip of rocky beach, a drop of some thirty feet below. Straight across lay the other shore of the Sound, just a low hunk of land, not looking like much at this distance—about eight miles across the water. The water was a glittering blue today, beautiful, with several sails visible upon it from where he watched. He should have suggested sailing to Jeannie; maybe she would have come.

She still seemed a kind of miracle to him; he could not get used to the new Jeannie, the girl grown up. The old comradeship was there between the two of them, but there was so much more besides. She was no longer a child, following him around; she was an adult, to whom he felt drawn not only by old ties, but by a likeness of character and feeling, the thing that had brought them together in the first place.

It had been the summer her parents died that he first saw Jeannie. She had been fourteen then. After the tragedy she had, of course, come to live with Jim and Marcia. He remembered her so well as she had looked then, a skinny girl, all eyes, elbows and knees, with her hair hanging in a skimpy ponytail down her back. From the front, with her hair pulled back from her face like that, she had looked almost like a boy. She had given little promise then of the beauty she had since become.

She had seemed so lost that summer, he remembered. There was not only her grief at her parents' sudden death, but the shock of being abruptly transplanted. Uprooted without warning from the Ohio town where she had grown up, removed from the house she had always lived in and from the friends she had known, she was a displaced person. Not that Jim and Marcia didn't do everything to make her feel welcome. But it was not the same as her own home, with her parents watching lovingly over her. And here in Rockton she had had no friends.

Tom had understood. He had been at the Townsends' practically every weekend that summer, and an instant rapport had sprung up between the two of them. How lonely a thing it was to go and live in someone else's house he knew from personal experience. He knew because it had happened to him. He had been eight when his mother had died and he had been taken to live with her unmarried sister. His father's job kept him away a great deal, and Dad had felt that he couldn't make a home for himself and his boy, much as he would have liked to. "It wouldn't be fair to you, Tom," he had said. "Aunt Frances can do much better for you than I can." So Dad had taken an apartment, and often as he had stayed with him, his home after that had been with Aunt Francie.

It had been this odd upbringing, he supposed, that had made him such a loner. He always felt separate from everyone in a way he didn't think most people experienced. He and his father were strangers, even; cut off from each other at such an early stage, they had been unable to build and maintain the close ties they should have had, and would have had, had they remained a family. Family life was the thing he missed. Aunt Francie loving and cherishing him was not the same thing. Relationships with people remained difficult for him—not with someone like Jim, of course, and other school friends he had had over the years. There it was easy: you liked the same things, such as tennis or football, and so you got along.

But marriage. That escaped him entirely. He knew nothing about it. No wonder he had made a mess of it. Girls he didn't understand in the first place. At college other fellows had occasionally fixed him up with a blind date. It had always been misery; he had been tongue-tied and had sat out the entire evening like a lump, unable even to make a start. He had become known at last at the frat house as "the monster," because no girl who'd been exposed to him would ever go out with him a second time: he was undatable.

So Betty had surprised him. To begin with she had teased him into taking her out. She was a secretary in the office next to his, worked for someone in the sales department, so that he had seen her daily and they had exchanged a few words. When he had finally asked her to dinner he had had no difficulty because she did all the talking. And after they were acquainted he found that it was, after all, possible for him to talk to a girl because by that time they seemed to be engaged. He couldn't to this day remember asking her, but he guessed he must have. Betty operated in such a highly-charged emotional atmosphere, though, that conversation at all times had been secondary. Most of what he could remember about her from that pre-marital period was physical.

He had no idea at what point he had made the discovery, but he knew now they should never, never have gotten married. Yet in retrospect it was difficult to determine when he could have called a halt. It had all gone forward inexorably from the beginning and one day he had found himself solidly wed. It had been a civil ceremony only, and soon afterwards they had made a trip to Baltimore so that he could introduce Betty to his family. She had hit it off fine with his father, though they hadn't spent much time with him; but she and Aunt Frances hadn't gotten on at all.

He had wanted to be married, once the prospect had come into view, he remembered that. To be part of a family, a real family, again, was something he had wanted ever since his mother died. But he didn't know enough about marriage, in fact knew practically nothing about it, so he no doubt idealized it. Anyhow what he and Betty had was not at all what he had expected. Until recently he had been putting its failure down to his own ineptitude. But for some time now he had wondered whether he were really wholly at fault. When he had blamed himself: "not cut out for marriage" hadn't he said to Marcia?—she had definitely disagreed with this diagnosis. And he respected Marcia's opinion. Marcia, in fact, was living proof that marriage could be a felicitous affair. She and Jim were happy, he knew that. And, trying to think about this thing honestly, apart from all the emotionalism in which he had become involved, he knew darn well that Marcia would never behave as Betty was behaving.

Squinting and gazing out across the water, he tried hard to think objectively about Betty and found himself contemplating a rather ugly picture. A feeling of bleakness crept over him and took possession, desiccating his spirit, as he faced up to the prospect of years and years ahead with his wife.

Something of which he had always been aware, of course, was that he felt sorry for Betty; that was one of the claims she had on him. Her blighted childhood made him feel guilty, for his, though half-orphaned, had at least been filled with love, and he could remember his mother, for he had had her when he was small and needed her most. But Betty. She hadn't even known who her parents were. Betty Miller, her name had been, but whether it was actually Miller or the name had just been parceled out to her so that she'd have one, she'd never been told. She'd been placed in one foster home after another, unloved, unwanted, her upkeep paid for by the city. In the last place she'd been they had mistreated her and she had finally run away. She'd had only part of a high school education; after she'd been on her own she'd worked as a waitress to pay for her secretarial courses. Later, when she had a job as a secretary, she had gone to night school and gotten her high school diploma and even taken some college courses. It had been a struggle. Because of all this he felt he should make allowances for Betty, and more than that, he had wanted to make it up to her for all the unhappiness she'd had.

Maybe if he took a firmer hand, as he had today when he'd told her they were not going to leave, things would be better. They would have to be if she were really pregnant.

Unaccountably, his thoughts turned to Jeannie. Twenty, she was, if he remembered correctly. He was eleven years older. She probably thought of him as over the hill, declining into middle age. Today he felt it: old, and tired, and most of all, empty.

He rose from the tussock of grass, dusting the sandy dirt from the seat of his pants. Mooning here by the seashore would get him nowhere. As he turned away from the prospect of sky and water he caught a glimpse far down the shore of a boy and girl walking hand in hand along the beach. Her hair blew in the wind. Young and carefree they were, he could tell by the way they moved. He trudged to the car, got in, and wearily switched on the engine.

Chapter 5

HARRY leaned against the door frame of his wife's bedroom, studying her as she slipped on a pair of aquamarine and pearl earrings. He had stopped just for a moment on his way downstairs to have a quick one before guests began to arrive.

Now he sauntered forward with the insolent slouch that showed he was in one of his more unpleasant moods. He stood in back of Karen as she sat at the satin-draped dressing table putting things back into the drawers and closing them.

He regarded her reflection in the mirror with distaste.

"Why don't you try bleaching your hair?" He lifted a lock of it, let it fall. "It might look less . . . less Mousy."

She ran a comb through the light brown strands, patted them into place. Her features weren't bad, really, just uninspired. They didn't, in fact, quite seem to belong together; yet it was a pleasant face, and when she smiled, which she was not doing now, almost pretty.

"Wherever did you get such an idea, Harry? I've always wished I really were a blonde, but I'm not going to do anything to change matters. It wouldn't be—well, it wouldn't be me."

"That's such a loss? Haven't you ever wanted to look different? Take Betty Graham. Don't you think she's stunning?"

Karen's eyes met his in the mirror, just for a moment. "She's striking—yes." He was just baiting her again, she knew. Harry had an eye for taste and quality and she was positive he would have put Tom's wife down as lacking either. To hold her up to his wife as a sample of what he admired was adding insult to injury, a refinement in technique which Harry would know was not lost upon her.

He smiled, but not to indicate any access of good humor. "You don't like her."

"I don't know her. But she seems—very nice." She wouldn't dream of saying what she really thought of Betty; she never said unkind things about people.

"That's damning with faint praise, for sure. But you'll admit she's got—well, say 'flair'."

"Oh, yes."

"Well that's what I'm talking about. If you just had more *flair*, Karen! Even your clothes." He shrugged. "I know you pay enough, but you ought to get things that dramatize you, make you look like somebody. That's the trouble. You look like a nobody. An absolute nobody."

The tears stood in her eyes now. She couldn't stop them. Her fingers fumbled with the stopper of the Chanel Number Five.

"The way you look, really, people must think I married you for your money."

"Well, didn't you?" The question came out in a stifled whisper.

His eyes lighted up for the first time since he had come into the room. "Ah, we have a little spirit after all, haven't we? You see, you *can* fight back."

"But I don't *like* to fight back. It makes me miserable!" She half turned on the velvet seat of the dressing table to look at him. "Harry, why do you torment me so? I don't understand it! I haven't done anything to you, I—"

"Of course you haven't. That's just it. You haven't done anything, you aren't anything. You're an utter blank. And if I torment you it's because I'm bored. Bored, bored, bored! What's the use of having all this money and no one to share it with but a blank? It spoils all the fun."

He turned away and sauntered toward the hall. At the door he pivoted on his heel. "Wear some diamonds. Slather them on. At least *look* expensive."

She held her tears until he had gone down the hall. And then they fell silently, the effort of holding them in making her shoulders tremble and her head ache suffocatingly.

He had indeed married her for her money, as she now knew. It had been so different before they were married! Harry had been gay, dashing, adoring. He had swept her off her feet. Handsome Harry, the fast-rising young man from Daddy's office. And she'd thought they would be so happy!

Harry had begun to show his discontent before the honeymoon was even ended. He had raged at her because she said she could do nothing to get her father to promote him faster; she had done what she could, but Mr. Kendrick had no intentions of making Harry a vice-president overnight, so to speak. Harry had gotten the title eventually, but when he did it hadn't satisfied him; he kept complaining that he was just a glorified office boy and shockingly underpaid, considering that he was the old man's son-in-law. Only son-in-law. And he had found fault with everything, especially with Karen. She had not known she was so flawed. It had never distressed her that she wasn't the prettiest girl in town; her friends had all liked her and she had always been popular. "Well, of course you were," Harry had said; "you had money."

Before they were married, she had put down Harry's streak of malice as a sense of humor—humor with a cutting edge, to be sure, but she hadn't supposed he meant the things he said; they were just for a laugh. Now she knew better. The laugh was there, certainly, but it was not good humor or gaiety that was its cause; it was his pleasure in the plunging in of the knife or the delicate flicking of its point against a sensitive skin that was for Harry the whole point of the joke.

Living with a perpetual detractor was demeaning. The things Harry said about other people did not distort her judgment of them; but as for herself, she had no source of reassurance. She thought of the happy, confident girl she had been at twenty-one; as Karen Kendrick, she had had everything. Only six years ago. She had been another person then.

She went into the bathroom and dabbed cold water on her eyes. They weren't too bad. She guessed a little eye shadow would help. She began to repair the damage.

"I'll drive over to the Judges'; my car's out in front anyway. O.K., Jim?"

It was the logical thing for Tom to take his car: no one, certainly, would want to go to a party in the Jaguar.

While they were assembling in the drive Jeannie came out the front door and joined them, a sweater over her arm and a clutch bag in her hand.

Tom swung toward her as though polarized.

"I thought you weren't coming?"

"So did I." She looked up at him quickly and away.

White again, thought Betty acidly. She knows she looks just wonderful in white, it sets her off, with that gorgeous tan.

They moved towards the car, Marcia explaining that she had been able, after all, to find someone to stay with the children. "I didn't want Jeannie to miss the party; she goes out seldom enough as it is."

"Oh, Marcia! You'd think I was becoming a recluse, the way you go on about me. It's just that my friends are scattered, now that they're mostly through college. They've all got jobs someplace."

"I guess we're lucky at that, to have you still at home," said Jim. "Why don't you marry Quint? We could keep you in the neighborhood."

"Oh, Jim, really! And I thought brothers improved with age!"

Tom's quick glance at Jeannie when Quint was mentioned was not lost on Betty. Ah, he *is* interested, she remarked to herself, whether he knows it or not. And the way he had brightened up when Jeannie appeared just now; at least she was forewarned. Luckily Tom was as transparent as a window pane; whatever went on, she would know it.

She thought back with nagging regret to the scene they had had this afternoon. She hadn't known what else to do, so had become really unpleasant in an effort to get them out of here. But it hadn't worked, and with the wisdom of hindsight she saw that she should have picked a different method to build a fire under Tom. It was unfortunate that she had ended up in such an unattractive role, yelling at him, she reflected ruefully, rather like a fishwife. The contrast between this picture of her and sweet little Jeannie might be doing a lot of damage at this very moment. As they got into the car she snuggled up to Tom; she must do what she could to restore her image—the right one.

Tom turned into the driveway to the Judges' house, a long, graveled curve commencing its sweep between a pair of massive stone gateposts. Betty recognized the place at once; she had often been past it. When the kids from Cressland wanted to park and neck they drove over here to the quiet byways where the rich lived. There was privacy along these dark residential roads: no street lights and a welcome scarcity of patrol cars, for trouble was not expected in the well-heeled, well-ordered bounds of Rockton.

So this was where Karen and Harry lived. The house was a great, sprawling mansion, dating probably from the twenties, when such English-style places had come into vogue. The grounds were beautiful. The lawns, in their setting amongst the surrounding woods, were neatly manicured, and at one end of the house, beyond the awning-covered terrace, there was even a putting green. Rhododendron and azaleas were banked against the walls, and scattered at intervals were clumps of ornamental trees—cut-leaf red maple, dogwood, crab-apple, weeping cherry. Where the drive turned in the circle by the entrance there was a rose garden.

They were greeted at the door by Karen, holding onto a big black and buff German shepherd who seemed determined to shake hands with everyone who came, and by Harry with a drink in his hand. The inside of the house was, if possible, even more impressive than the exterior. This place made Marcia's look like a cottage, thought Betty with an inner smirk of satisfaction. Everywhere were genuine antiques—things bought in Europe or from the best sources in New York; art objects collected over the years from the finest galleries; oil paintings worth a fortune. As she made her way into the ballroom-sized drawing room, a story and a half high and filled with more expensive furniture and wall-to-wall oriental rugs, she felt a stab of pure covetousness. This was wealth. If you had this kind of place you had everything: the servants that went with it, the cars, a yacht if you wanted one, a place in Florida or the Bahamas.

They were not the first guests. Betty repressed a shudder at the recollection summoned up at sight of Peggy and Chuck Bennett standing halfway down the long room. All she could think of was Peggy, gasping for breath like a drowning person, her large, red mouth opening and closing over the rush of words. "Someone

dead in the drive. Oh, it's *horrible!* Just lying there!"
And all the time there had been on her face the pleased
quirk of a smile, that inexplicable tinge of joy in the
imparting of dread news to those who had not heard it.
And there was Peg now, brightening at their arrival,
ready to worry the carcass of last night's tragedy with
all the pleasure of a terrier who has found a dead rab-
bit.

Betty, with Marcia, approached the Bennetts on an
angle so that she could slide on by, and after a brief exchange of remarks she turned away leaving Marcia to
give the two of them a rundown on what the police had
been doing today.

She wandered to the far end of the room, looking at
the oils on the walls, a tapestry, a collection of Chinese
porcelain, some carved ivory pieces, assorted objects in-
laid with mother-of-pearl, and a seemingly endless va-
riety of ornamental bric-a-brac. Having reached the
grand piano which stood in a corner near one of the
doors to the awninged terrace, she leaned forward in
the late afternoon gloom to see the framed photographs
displayed on the closed top of the instrument.

"The rogues' gallery," said a voice behind her and
she started, for she had not heard Harry Judge's footsteps on the oriental rug.

"Oh, hello." She pivoted, and leaning back against
the piano gave him one of her most attractive smiles.

"What can I get you to drink, Betty?"

"Oh, a martini, please."

She felt a trifle let down that he left her so promptly to get it; she wanted someone to talk to. She watched him as he stopped to speak for a moment to Jim. At the far end of the room Quint Rutledge had just come in and was chatting with Tom and Jeannie. That little snip! Hadn't she understood she was to stay away from Tom?

Betty smoothed away a frown as Jim, catching sight of her all alone by the piano, ambled over to keep her company. His big frame seemed quite in scale with the over-sized room.

"Ready for a hair of the dog, by now?" she asked, twitting him good-humoredly.

"Lord, no!" He passed a hand over his broad forehead. "I told Harry to bring me a double highball glass of water with an eyedropper-full of Scotch. And I'm going to nurse it all evening."

"Sure you're not over-reacting?"

"After yesterday?" His voice splintered on the words and she felt a spurt of surprise. Till this moment it had not occurred to her that Jim Townsend could be seriously worried about his own neck; people with money, living in nice houses in towns like Rockton were secure, weren't they? But because he had been drinking and had passed out in the den Jim had no alibi for the time of Mrs. Wiebald's death.

With wry amusement she changed the subject. "What a gorgeous house this is."

"Yes, big enough. You could play hockey in here. It's the Kendrick place. Karen's dad had it built when he was a young man, back when huge houses like this were still being built. Karen and Harry moved in after his death; everything came to Karen, naturally: only child, you know, and Mrs. Kendrick's been dead for years."

Jim stepped aside and their twosome became a triangle as Quint joined them, bowing to Betty in the off-hand courtly way he had.

"We were just discussing Harry's spread here." Jim gestured towards the rest of the vast living room.

"Yes, he's fallen heir to quite an establishment. Just what he always wanted, I think, too." Quint gazed up at the dark beams against the white, vaulted ceiling. "I can't imagine what anyone wants with a tremendous place like this. Karen likes it, of course, because she grew up here." This last he seemed to be saying mostly to himself.

"I suppose you grew up somewhere around here, too?" Betty asked. Not that she was really much interested in knowing.

"Oh, yes; local boy, definitely."

She was glad to see Harry returning, a drink in either hand. She would so much rather talk to him than to these two—one very dull husband and one very sharp lawyer to whom she had taken an acute dislike.

Quint's brilliant eyes rested on Betty, giving her again the feeling that he could see her backbone from the front. "And where did *you* come from, Betty?"

She hesitated, casting about for a convenient answer, one that would not lead to another question and another.

"Out of a pumpkin," said Harry lightly, smiling, and handed her a martini.

A small laugh rippled around the little circle. Jim, who had been only half listening, took the tall, very pale highball Harry had brought him and turned away with it to greet a pair of new arrivals. Betty had laughed with the others, but now dismay seeped through the relief she had momentarily felt at being off the hook.

"Didn't you, now?" Harry ran his hand along her arm familiarly. She was shocked. Not shocked that he had done it, she had been expecting him to make more of a pass soon; but the fact that he had done it with Quint watching really alarmed her. He must have expected her to take it and say nothing.

She became aware that Quint Rutledge's queer eyes with their little tic were watching her with even greater interest than before; he'd missed nothing. Nor had he lost the thread of the conversation.

"How fortunate," he murmured, "that Tom happened to have the glass slipper." With that parting remark he left them.

And now she stood alone with Harry.

"Where *do* you hail from, my dear?" The dark eyes were amused, taunting. Yet something more underlay the amusement: a threat. She felt it unmistakably. Oh, yes; if she had had any doubt, it was gone: Harry knew who she was. And she was certain, too, as certain now as if she had seen him put it in the envelope, that it was Harry who had sent her the clipping.

Summoning her scattered resources to repel the attack, she stared boldly up into his face. She had the answer: she need only take what he had said and give it a twist of her own.

"Well, you were almost right, you know; only not Cinderella. Ella Cinders. Or didn't you read comic strips when you were a boy?"

As Harry threw back his head, laughing with genuine delight, Betty's gaze was drawn to the portrait hanging over the massive fireplace. She stared, mesmerized, while all the chips seemed to fall into place.

It was an excellent painting. The artist went beyond photographic likeness to portray the full personality of the subject. This was undoubtedly Mr. Kendrick. And the last time she had seen him there had been a small trickle of blood running down his forehead, but he was not seriously hurt. In fact, all he'd asked for was help to get up from the crazy tilt of the train seat . . .

Harry stood watching Jim, who looked like the original fall guy. Really, those football players usually were as dumb as you'd expect. He was bending over Jeannie as she sat next to Karen talking about dogs (as he could hear) and patting Rolfe on the head. Jeannie was one he could definitely do without. She didn't like him, he knew. He had caught her on more than one previous occasion looking at him as if he were something to be squashed underfoot. Someday he was going to get back at her, make her realize what a mistake she was making. If she only knew him better she'd appreciate him, he was sure of that. Damn good looking she was, and that annoyed him. What she really needed, he thought, was a good raping. It would be a pleasure.

The party tonight seemed interminable. He was still racking his brains to think of some way to deal with Betty. Whatever she knew or didn't know, it was still too much for safety. Oddly enough, she didn't seem too much afraid of him; in fact, she gave him the impression she felt she'd at last met her match. Could she be so besotted with her own charms that she really thought she'd be able to buy him off with the promise of a fleshly alliance? Well, if that was the case let her think it; it would keep her mouth shut while he figured things out. And anything she wanted to give away in the line of favors would be a welcome windfall.

The cocktail hour flowed on. The guest list this evening was almost the same as last night's party; two couples had been added, new to the Grahams, and one at a time they cased the guests of honor. Karen spent a long time talking to Betty, perhaps to gave the lie to Harry's accusation that she didn't like her.

"Do you have children, Karen?" Betty put the question with a polite but vacant smile suggesting that her thoughts were elsewhere.

Harry, half listening as he poured himself another drink, saw the inevitable stricken look and the covert glance in his direction, a silent reproach. Damn it, why should he be expected to put up with a bunch of wailing, runny-nosed kids, making a mess of the house, just to please her? "Don't you want a son, Harry? Think how much he would mean to you." A son to follow in his footsteps, a pushing kid, hating his guts, ready to grab it all, just waiting to shove his old man out? Oh, no.

"No, we haven't any." Karen reached out instinctively to lay her hand on the head of the dog Rolfe, who sat on his haunches at her knee, his tongue lolling out, his bright attention shifting from guest to guest as he enjoyed the party. The warm life under her fingers was reassuring. Ninety pounds of affection pressed against her leg.

"Well, I'm with you," Betty said, through dearth of interest missing altogether the tone of Karen's reply. "I don't see why everyone wants a clutch of offspring. If you ask me, it's the grand delusion of the postwar world. Women are making brood sows of themselves. I think it's most unattractive."

"Well, you're a newlywed, of course. I'm willing to bet that in a few years you'll change your mind."

"Or Tom'll change it for me?" Her eyes sought out her husband across the room. No, he wasn't with Jeannie, he was talking to one of the Judges' neighbors that they'd just met, a middle-aged woman with a lot of teeth and brown hair that was gray at the part.

Dinner was served on the awninged terrace, where a white-jacketed colored man presided over a buffet table. Three round tables with pink linen cloths accommodated the guests and their plates. Betty, seated on one of the white metal chairs, unfolded the pink napkin on her lap and took note of the pink centerpiece of roses and snapdragons with a pang of envy akin to actual pain. This was how one should live. How lucky Karen was. Yet on her all this was wasted; she seemed a girl of simple tastes who didn't even appreciate what her money could buy.

Harry was seated next to her, and from time to time during dinner she felt his hand on her leg, under the tablecloth. When she fidgeted his dark eyes were upon her in sardonic amusement, and then his fingers grasped hers hard in a warning to sit still and say nothing. By now it was abundantly clear to Betty that she was his target for an affair. At the thought her nerve endings tingled. It was not altogether an unpleasant prospect. She had never had an affair. There had been Tom before they were married, but she had thought of that definitely as a prelude to matrimony, not really to be classified as a liaison. She had always wondered what it would be like to have one. Exciting, perhaps wildly exciting. She would like, of course, to have chosen the time, the place, and the man; now she was having the terms dictated to her. And not only was there the threat of discovery by her husband, there was also the threat of instant exposure by Harry, should he choose to do that to her. She must see that she was an unqualified success, make herself indispensable to Harry, so that he would never for a moment toy with the idea of telling what he knew.

It was sometime after dinner that Harry made his move. Some of the party were still on the terrace, where candles flickered now in the bottoms of green glass containers, and others had gone into the living room where one of their number was playing recent song hits on the piano. Harry took her through the living room, down a hall, and into a small paneled library, where he turned on a couple of lamps with a wall switch and closed the door behind him.

"Well," he said. "I've been waiting for this."

"So have I." Her heart hammered and she heard her own words as if someone else had spoken them.

"I see you got my letter; or do you always take up with other men so easily?"

Resentment almost flared, but she quashed it—instantly. She mustn't forget that he held the whip hand.

"I got your letter. Otherwise things wouldn't have gone *this* fast, attractive as you are."

He sucked in his lower lip and studied her. "Well, now, you needn't lick my boots; you might only get a kick in the teeth. That wouldn't be as much fun for either of us."

A bright spot burned in either cheek; she could feel them. "Don't worry, I wouldn't be any good at boot-licking. I've had no practice. When I said you were attractive I was giving you the truth for its value to you; you wouldn't like to think, would you, that you've only forced my interest with a threat?"

She had said the right thing. Admiration kindled in his face, guardedly; he would never give her the satisfaction of truly revealing his feelings to her, but she could read enough there to continue, encouraged, on the same tack.

"No," he conceded, wondering what she would say next, "that I wouldn't."

"The fact is, till you came along I thought I was satisfied with Tom."

"Um. 'Satisfied' is such a dull condition. It's scarcely better than 'dissatisfied,' for my money."

"How about 'unsatisfied'?" she asked huskily. As they stood there face to face he saw undisguised hunger in her face, hunger for him. The look in her eyes was as physical as a touch and to his surprise it had a physical effect on him. He hadn't expected that. In fact he had never experienced anything quite like it: the girl was a witch.

He took himself sharply in hand. "Unsatisfied?" It seemed a long time ago that she had said that. "That's where we are now, isn't it?"

"I hope so. And I'm afraid from the look of you that you could keep a girl unsatisfied a long time—even if you gave her everything she asked."

"And why is that?"

"Because you're a devil. You're being a devil right now; you're trying to force me to make the first move—even if you don't like bootlickers. Isn't that so?"

"Could be." It was all he could do to keep his hands off her.

"Well, I'll make the first move." She put her hands on his shoulders, slid her arms around his neck and brushed her lips lightly across his until his mouth came down upon hers like a bruise.

My God! she thought, straining against him. What she had told Harry was true, but she hadn't known it till this moment: she *had* been satisfied with Tom, but no longer. Tom was dull, dull, dull! It was Harry who was exciting. The danger added to it, in some occult way, raised the thrill to a higher power.

"I think we've got a good thing here," he murmured to her. "How about you?"

"Do you really need to ask?" She gave him another

liquid gaze, guaranteeing that inside she was passion unalloyed.

He flipped out the lights, and "unsatisfied" became an understatement. He was a man with a raging thirst.

"Look," he said. They'd been missing from the party long enough now. Too long. "I want more than this. When can I see you alone?"

With an effort, her head far from clear, she said, "Tomorrow—maybe." She tried to think. "Tom tells me we're invited to go sailing on Jeannie's boat while the rest of them are at church. I can beg off with a head-ache."

"You do that." He ran his hands over her again in the dark, ending up by squeezing her shoulders so hard that she gave a muffled gasp. "That's just to let you know that I can play rough if you cross me. Very rough; you wouldn't like it."

"Why would I cross you?"

"Well, I wouldn't recommend it. One wrong move, Mrs. Melinder—how's Al, by the way?" He was glad to feel her flinch under his fingers at her husband's name. He would get in a few demoralizing strokes be-fore he let her go, something to tide her over until to-morrow.

"I won't make one wrong move. I'm in your camp now; why should I?"

"And you're going to be a good little camp follower. That it?"

"I don't like a label like that."

"I can do worse than pin a label on you, don't forget."

"I almost did forget—a few minutes ago. Can't we drop the threat business? It got me into your arms, but once I was there—oh, Harry!" She moved up against him again and ran her finger down his cheek. "I've never met anyone like you. The others were all dogs—just dogs!"

"Even Tom?"

"Yes, Tom."

"What a nice tribute." He wasn't going to let her charms take hold again. "But I want no mistake made: you're going to keep your mouth shut?"

"Of course." In the darkness she gave a puzzled frown. "What have I got to open my mouth about? You know everything about me; all I know about you is what we haven't done yet—that's tomorrow, maybe."

So she *didn't* know, he thought swiftly. Or was smart enough to pretend she didn't. She was a cool one; she was quite capable of acting the innocent because she knew how dangerous a little knowledge could be. Well, he wouldn't let slip anything she didn't already know.

He smiled sweetly at her. "I worry about my wife, you see. You understand? She cries all the time when she finds out things like this. We just needn't upset her —need we?"

She lifted one corner of her lips. "I think it's sweet

of you to be so thoughtful. And too bad Karen isn't able to appreciate it. You must be a model philanderer."

"I try. What time tomorrow? Eleven? That's church time, I think. Just right for commandment breaking."

A tremor passed down her spine at this last light remark. Betty's family had been churchgoers and she had spent every childhood Sunday morning in a pew hearing about the punishments of the wicked. "All right. Eleven."

Harry turned on the light, which seemed terribly bright after the long interval of darkness. Her hand went quickly to her hair to smooth it back.

"Your lipstick needs fixing. Next door beyond this one off the hall."

"So does yours," she flashed. "It's all over you."

As she opened the door he was pulling out his handkerchief. The hall was empty and she slipped unseen into the bedroom with its roomy bath next door. To her relief she found lipsticks, powder, and perfume lined up on the dressing table. That was lucky, because she had left her handbag in the living room—along with a few intangibles that she had walked irrevocably away from with Harry Judge.

Karen had paused, one hand on the outside door of the sun porch, the other grasping Rolfe by the collar, as Quint came up behind her.

"He's getting to be a nuisance; he thinks the party's for him."

"Yes, I noticed him joining in, sitting on the sofa beside the guests and so on."

"Big lummox. It's my own fault for making a lap dog out of him. I'll put him in his yard."

"Let me. It's dark out there."

"Oh, I'm all right."

Quint held the door and together they led the big German shepherd out to the gate of the chain link enclosure. Karen pushed down the fastener and they turned back towards the lighted house.

The darkened lawn where they stood was adjacent to the library, its lamp-lit interior clearly visible. Quint had started to say something, but his voice faded away. "Karen, I wanted to—"

He stopped dead. There was no mistaking the two people within. The girl stood with her hand on the man's arm and as they watched from the damp grass the two in the library kissed. Harry's hands slid over her body with obviously no expectation on his part of a rebuff.

Quint drew Karen aside where she could no longer see.

"It makes no difference, Quint." Her voice sounded suffocated. "That's nothing new."

Silently he took her hand and pressed it.

She looked up at him in the dim light that streamed out to them from the house, slatting across the grass.

"Did you only date me, Quint, because of my money?"

His fingers dug into her shoulder so hard it hurt. "You know better than that. What—"

"Harry says so."

He gave a strangled exclamation. "Oh, he does, does he?" His hand tightened on hers. "Why do you think I've remained unmarried all this time? Do I really have to spell it out for you? Because the one dear, sweet person I wanted married Harry Judge and because I—oh, hell!"

"Oh." Her voice was stifled. "It wasn't fair of me to ask you Quint dear. Only I'd begun to doubt that anyone *ever* wanted me for myself—the way Harry talks, you know—and I'd begun to think he might be right."

"Don't listen to him; he judges everything by his own lights, and they're dim indeed. You mean he says things like *that* to you?"

"I can't help but listen; I live with him."

"Listen, Karen. Any time you feel like calling it quits with Harry, I'm here. And I don't mean just legal assistance. It's not my kind of game to try to break up another man's marriage, but damn his soul, Harry deserves every effort I can bend in that direction."

"Oh, Quint, no!" She put her other hand over his and

123

looked up at this tall, kind man who was apparently still hers for the asking. "I'm sorry. I started all this with my stupid question—and unkind it was, too—"

"No it wasn't. I'm glad to have broken silence."

"But Quint, it's no good, you see. No use. I still love Harry. I can't imagine why, it's nothing I can do anything about."

"It's generally not something we can do anything about." But maybe she won't always feel that way, he couldn't help thinking.

"Let's go in," he said, an arm about her shoulders. He was more shaken by their interchange than he would care to admit, even to himself. He had supposed that long ago he had abandoned all hope; that tired of chasing girls, he had really settled down in semi-contentment to bachelorhood, his natural state. But it seemed that this was not true at all. Just that question of Karen's had done it. "Did you only date me because of my money?" and his answer, which had been ready and waiting and he hadn't known it. He felt as if he had a raw, new wound in his chest.

They stood at the edge of the living room. "Poor Jeannie," said Quint. "She's having a rough time just now." He smiled at Karen and left her to wend his way over to the object of his concern.

Jeannie having a rough time? It was the first Karen had heard of it. She watched the two of them for a moment, the tall, lithe, gray-haired figure bent to speak to the young girl, the lovely young face looking up in welcome. Karen was gripped by a sudden feeling of panic. What if Quint should marry Jeannie? Oh, you dog in the manger! she reprimanded herself.

But she depended on him so.

Keith Shaffer, the Judges' neighbor from across the road, was still playing the piano—old favorites now, songs popular in the thirties and forties. Tom leaned against the long side of the instrument, a concert grand, listening to the music and talking to Jim. His eyes rested on Jeannie, seated on a brocade sofa under the brooding clouds of a dark-toned landscape massively framed in gold. It depressed him that she was talking to Quint. Not that he didn't like Quint—he was one of the best. But he was too old for her. Tom brought himself up short as he thought this, and tried to visualize Jeannie talking with a younger man, say one about twenty-two. No, that would be even worse: he could hardly bear the thought.

He wondered now where Betty was. He thought she had come inside, but he must have been mistaken because he didn't see her in here. She was probably still out on the terrace, from whence laughter and the burr of conversation drifted in through the two pairs of French doors. Apparently Betty was sorry about the quarrel this afternoon; she'd been trying this evening to make it up to him, letting him know by little signals that things were all right between them now. Yet instead of happiness at this restoration of harmony he felt merely relief. Indeed, what he had taken for happiness in his early days with Betty had been, he long since realized, for the most part only surcease from loneliness; and even that had been laced through with so many threads of discord that he would have welcomed back the loneliness, with its peace and quiet.

He'd always heard that the first year of marriage was the hardest—the year in which the rough edges were worn off two people so that they fitted at last into a unified whole; he hadn't expected things to get worse instead of better. After the first two months they certainly had. Those early weeks had been semi-happy while they had been on their honeymoon, and then the time when they were just settling down in the apartment. Though even then he had never known when Betty, in one of her mercurial moods, would fling off in a rage at something he didn't even know he'd done. At least the reconciliations had been quick and warm. The whole thing had been like a ride on a roller coaster.

Well, as he'd decided this afternoon, he'd take a firm hand and hope for the best. If there was one thing this weekend visit had shown him, it was that he was not nearly so much at fault as he had believed, in the failure their marriage had become. Seeing Betty among his friends he had for the first time seen her in perspective. And reluctant as he had been to recognize the fact, he knew that she did not stack up well in the estimation of his peers. He was not one who had ever cared what other people thought: he would hold to his own opinion in the face of any opposition. But here, where he could sense that one by one his friends had weighed Betty and found her wanting, and that this estimation matched the conclusion he himself had subconsciously reached but fought against accepting —well, the verdict was in and he would make the best he could of it. Everyone had been more than kind; he could see Marcia, see Jim, make the extra effort to be nice to Betty when they didn't like her. He could do no less; he would have to do much more. Because it still came down to one important fact, and one of the facts which had brought him to marriage—that he felt so sorry for her. He wouldn't have thought that at first; she had seemed so glamorous, so sure of herself, no one would have believed her an object to be pitied. But when you got more than skin deep there it was: she was an unhappy person with a history of unhappiness.

And don't go whitewashing your motives for marrying her, he told himself bitterly. The biggest single reason was lust. Good old-fashioned lust. He hadn't known it wasn't love. Fool's gold, looking so like the real. He looked at the real again, sitting next to Quint, and tried to stanch the flow of tenderness that welled up in him. You're only making yourself miserable, he told himself fruitlessly; don't look at her. Maybe Betty was right: they should get out of here.

"Enjoying the party?" Quint said to her.

"Of course." Jeannie smiled absently.

He studied her. Then he reached out and touched her wrist. "May I give you some fatherly advice?"

She looked up sharply, almost afraid, he thought. "If you like."

"You're riding for a fall. You know that don't you?"

"Tell me about it." She gazed at him steadily.

"Well naturally you know there's no future in it."

"In what?" She leaned forward, begging him to go on. He didn't know whether to be impatient with her or not, and decided not. She wasn't that dense.

"You *do* know what I'm talking about—"

She nodded. "I just wanted you to say it."

"All right. Tom." She closed her eyes at the name, but smiled ever so slightly as though the sound of it gave her both pleasure and pain.

Quint looked at her in alarm. She was farther gone than he'd thought. "Good God," he said roughly, almost under his breath. His fingers bit into the flesh of her upper arm. "Now I've *got* to talk to you. Come outside."

With a sinking heart Karen watched them go. Arm around her, Quint took Jeannie out the front door into the privacy of darkness. Well, thought Karen, she had sent him away. She had told him she still loved Harry. She did. But—

Tom also watched them go. Jim's words had stuck with him, his bantering remark to Jeannie: "Why don't you marry Quint?" At this moment he hated Quint—single, and alone with Jeannie somewhere out there.

They sat on a little white iron seat, with leaves and scrolls across its back, at the edge of the rose garden.

"Do you really have it as bad as that, Jeannie?"

"I'm afraid so."

"Well take yourself in hand, then. You *can't* fall in love with Tom Graham; he's married. You're not that kind of girl."

"Yes, I know. Don't you think I've been telling myself that? But it's too late. It was too late yesterday. I didn't know or I'd have gone away for the weekend. I mean I didn't know how I'd feel. You see, Tom was my first big crush—ever. When I first came here, he used to come out every weekend. I was sort of lost then. Mother and Dad had just been killed and I was so lonely. I missed my friends. It's hard, you know, to move suddenly to a new place—I didn't know anyone here but Jim and Marcia. Tim was a baby then, and Marcia busy with him—and she and Jim were so happy; I felt like an interloper, even though they were very sweet to me.

"It was Tom who knew how I felt; he patted me on the head and made me feel better. I hung onto him, I guess. And you know how girls that age are; no, I guess you don't. Well, they can be deadly serious about love. Tom didn't know it, but I was head over heels in love with him, that year and the next. He thought of me as just a kid, of course. Which I was.

"The second summer I was here Jim bought me that dinghy, and Tom taught me to sail it. We spent days out on the water together. I still felt the same about him: he was the most important thing in my life.

"Then he got that job in Chicago, and I haven't seen him since, till now. And believe me, Quint, it was a shock to find that I was still in love with him. I thought I'd laid the whole thing away in lavender, another memory pressed into my book of same—just a keepsake of my youth. Then yesterday, wham! As soon as I saw him. And I'm a big girl, now; it's different from when I was fifteen."

"Well you can't let it take you like that."

"That's nice advice, Quint. But when a thing has roots in the past, roots that go so deep, you can't just tear it out. You know that."

"Yes, I know that." His voice was sad. She knew he was thinking of Karen.

"At least Tom doesn't know how I feel, and I'll see that he doesn't."

"Then you'll have to try harder than you're trying now. Every time you look at him it's as if you'd just been turned on—like a light."

"That bad? And I wondered how you'd guessed."
She sounded dispirited.

"What's your prognosis for the future, little dear?"

"You mean will I get over it?" Suddenly she pressed
her face against the sleeve of his jacket. "Oh, Quint,
what will I do?" The note of utter despair, coming
without warning, touched him. He put an arm around
her. "The awful thing is that I don't *want* to get over
it! If I did I think I'd die! It would be like cutting my
heart out." The last words were choked out and he felt
her holding her breath as she tried to stop the sobs from
beginning.

He kissed the top of her head, comforting her as
though she were a child. But she broke from him and
walked away. He didn't know that it was the feel of his
arms around her that she found unbearable: the wrong
arms, the wrong man.

After a moment she turned back to him.

"I'm all right now. Goodness, Quint, I'm sorry. All
those melodramatics." Even in the dark, he could see
that she made a face.

"You sound better," he said, relieved.

"Well it helps to talk to someone. I've had it bottled
up inside me. Obviously there hasn't been a soul I could
unburden myself to. You're a godsend."

"Now that's the nicest thing anyone's said to me in a
long time."

"And thanks. I'll try to take your advice. If I can stay away from him it'll help."

"His wife is likely to cut you to ribbons if you don't —unless she's too busy elsewhere."

But she didn't hear the last of his remark. Frowning, she sat down again.

"She's already tried. She—"

Jeannie hesitated. Should she tell him about it?

"What do you mean, she's tried?"

"She threatened me. First it wasn't about Tom, though, it was about a letter. A letter came for her in the mail today and I handed it to her. Later on she came looking for me and told me she knew I'd sent it and not to try to frighten her."

"*What?*"

"That's what she said. And she said it wouldn't work, I wasn't pushing her out. Something like that. And then, Quint—see what you make of this: she said something about Mrs. Wiebald, and if I understood her correctly she said 'It could happen to you.' "

For some moments Quint sat perfectly still. Then he said, in a voice whose urgency sent a chill over her: "Listen, Jeannie. Keep away from her. She's either completely off her rocker or she's a girl in serious trouble, with God knows what behind it."

"You really think so? I thought maybe I was going off half-cocked when I got so worried over it."

"If she said what you think she said, no explanation

is possible but one of the utmost gravity. At the very best she's being either threatened or blackmailed. And could be she's involved in the killing of Mrs. Wiebald—though I shouldn't think she'd admit such a thing to you."

"That's what I thought: if she'd killed her she certainly wouldn't say so. I had the feeling that she was perhaps just saying that—that something could happen to me—to scare me into leaving her alone. Though what she thought I was threatening her with I don't know. I do know she ascribed a motive to me. She said she knew I was trying to get Tom for myself."

"She doesn't miss much. And Tom's her bread and butter—or should I say cake and caviar. I have reason to believe she doesn't care a fig for him as far as love, honor, and so forth come into it—"

"How do you know that?" She laced her fingers together and pressed the palms tight, almost in an attitude of prayer.

"Never mind. And don't go building anything on it, either. I shouldn't have told you that much. Take my advice, dear Jeannie, and stay well away from the Grahams, both husband and wife. I think a very ugly mess may be shaping up."

"Poor Tom. You mean she doesn't even *love* him?"

"Let's drop that angle of it, shall we? I just know she's a number one bitch. And from what you tell me she may be worse. I think her past history will bear a little looking into. I may have a client to clear, you know: your brother. So anything I can find—"

"Jim's really in trouble?" Alarm crept over her, quickening her pulse, tightening her throat.

"I hope not. Nothing official yet. But it was his car, his fingerprints on the wheel, and he can't prove by anyone that he was in the den at the time Mrs. Wiebald was killed."

Jeannie grasped his sleeve with both hands. "I think Mrs. Wiebald knew something about Betty."

"You're guessing? Or what?"

"Betty said it herself. We were all three in the kitchen just before Mrs. Wiebald left the house. Betty came in kind of suddenly—looking for Tom, she said— and remarked that wasn't it odd our sitter had this idea that she—Betty—looked like somebody she used to know."

"My God. And the woman was killed just after that. Did she say anything to Betty—Mrs. Wiebald?"

"No. She just shut up suddenly—not like her, I thought at the time, because she was always such a great gabber. She just shut up and left."

"I *will* be damned. Did you tell the police any of this?"

"No. What Mrs. Wiebald had said about Betty completely slipped my mind after she was killed. And at the time the police were questioning us last night it wouldn't have seemed worth mentioning even if I'd thought of it. It's only in connection with what happened this afternoon—the talk about the threatening letter, and Betty threatening me—that Mrs. Wiebald's remark assumes possible importance. And Quint, you know that none of it's the sort of thing I could bring myself to volunteer to the police anyway: I'd feel I was trying to incriminate Betty, and I can't *do* that."

"From what you've told me I'd think she hardly deserves such consideration. Hm. Well, I'll be talking to Captain Fellini tomorrow and I'll pass these little tidbits on to him. If he comes out to question you you'll tell him what you know?"

"I'd have to, wouldn't I?"

"That's right, you'd have to. And I'm going to get some quiet investigation under way myself, see what I can find out about our little Mrs. Graham."

They rose and made their way across the drive and up the short brick walk to the entrance. Quint smiled down at her. "We've certainly been out here long enough to start the best grade of gossip."

"They just can't stand seeing anyone stay single, can they! Jim keeps trying to marry me off to you."

"If I had any sense I'd ask you; or any feelings left where they're supposed to be."

"I guess neither of us has any sense." But she said it gaily enough, and he was glad to see in the light of the front entrance that she looked quite unscathed by her bout with emotion.

Was it really any better to be young and unhappy than to be middle-aged and unhappy? Perhaps it was easier at his age; by now he was used to it.

The evening was coming to a close. Several of the guests had left already, including Quint, who had taken Jeannie home. The Grahams lingered near the big, ornate fireplace, its hearth at this season aglow with summer flowers instead of its winter flames. Betty was repaying Karen's hospitality with a few kind words, overdoing it just a little and taking particular pleasure in congratulating her hostess on a happiness she knew did not exist. This pallid woman could never have been in tune with Harry. The memory of his savage caresses brought a sparkle to her eyes and a warmth to her voice as she talked so pleasantly with his wife, knowing that she was one up on her in every way except money. The fire she had kindled with Harry was something the like of which Karen had never felt.

"You and Harry must be so *happy* with a wonderful place like this . . . this marvelous house!" Betty's glance roved over some of the nearer art treasures.

"Oh, I grew up here," said Karen deprecatingly. "I guess I'm used to it. Though it's a little big for just the two of us."

Betty's protuberant eyes rested on the portrait over the mantel. "That's your father, I expect?"

"Yes, that's Dad, painted not long before the . . .

the train accident. It's still hard to believe he's . . .
I miss him, you know."

"You must have been so thankful Harry wasn't killed
in the wreck." Betty was pleased that she sounded so
sympathetic. But when she looked from old Mr.
Kendrick to Karen the latter was staring at her in surprise.

"Oh, *Harry* wasn't on the train with my father."

"He wasn't?" Betty opened her mouth a little
stupidly. In the moment before she looked at Harry, a
premonition of catastrophe hovered over her like the
reputed stillness preceding an earthquake.

Then the ground seemed to open up in great fissures
before her and she thought she might fall. Her eyes
reached his and now she was feeling his anger, silent
and dreadful, reaching across the intervening space and
curling to charred nothing the tendrils of passion he
had caused to take root within her. Her marriage to
Tom, and all she had gained with it, seemed to be sift-
ing in ashes to her feet.

Almost imperceptibly Harry shook his head. *That*
was what she was supposed to keep her mouth shut
about: not their clandestine lovemaking, but the train,
the damned, bloody train. Just as a drowning person is
supposed to see his entire life in an instant's recapitula-
tion, so the whole sequence of events connected with
Harry Judge flashed by in its true, lurid colors.

"I was lucky," he was saying in a matter-of-fact way.

He had stepped forward to stand now, his arm linked through his wife's in a travesty of connubial solidarity. "I was in New York with Melvin that day, but I stayed in the city for dinner instead of taking the train out with him. Just luck."

"Yes, how lucky!" echoed Betty, searching his face now for signposts to point her way. But she could read nothing from his expression; he was just a man standing with his wife and making polite conversation with the departing guests.

Tom was thanking Karen for the lovely time, while Jim and Marcia, laughing over something, lingered in the entrance hall waiting for them.

A few minutes later they trekked out the door to the car. Then it was that Harry took her hand, in the darkness at the edge of the drive, and squeezed it so viciously, grinding the bones together, that she thought she would scream.

"Well, little Mrs. Graham!" he exclaimed, the very picture of the jovial host. "It's been a pleasure. And come to think of it, I haven't kissed the bride, have I?" And in the manner customary among men kissing publicly the wives of their friends, he bent over her.

"I'll see you tomorrow, doll," he murmured. The kiss was not the kind usually bestowed on the wife of a friend, and left her trembling with its violence. She had just one glimpse of his eyes in the light from inside, and they were cruel and black.

As the car bore them away into the darkness of the trees and through the shadowy gateposts, from some frightened quarter of her mind came the chill of premonition.

Tom, at the wheel, turned to her, feeling her shiver. "You're cold."

"Yes." The voice was faint. "I think I'm coming down with something."

Chapter 6

"I'M SORRY you don't feel up to it," said Jeannie. "We'll go another time when you're here."

After Quint's warnings of the night before she had debated what to do about taking the Grahams out for a sail and had concluded that the matter was out of her hands. She couldn't uninvite them.

But just now Betty had stopped her in the upstairs hall to convey her regrets. She didn't feel well.

"Just not seaworthy. Or would that be the boat?" Her friendly manner was in marked contrast to the tenor of yesterday's verbal exchange.

"Can I get something for you?" Jeannie went on, after saying how sorry she was. "Aspirin or anything?"

"Thanks. I'll be all right if I just stay off the water. I'm sure it would make me queasy."

"Well, then Tom won't want to go either of course—"

"Oh, Tom's still going."

"But—"

"I wouldn't think of his missing the chance; he loves the water."

Jeannie could hardly believe her ears. "Well if you're sure." She studied the handsome, carefully made-up face, its too-sure look like a hard edge. "After what you said to me yesterday—"

"Yesterday I was wrong. And I apologize." Betty laid a hand on her arm. "Please believe me when I say how sorry I am. I'm glad you set me straight about the letter; as it happens I know now who sent it. And it was nothing to worry Tom about, so don't you mention it to him either, if you don't mind. It was a sort of private joke—from a—friend of mine."

"Oh, I see." But from Betty's expression it must not have been a particularly amusing joke, at that. "Well I'm glad you solved the mystery. Do you know for sure that Tom still wants to go without you?"

"He'll go. I want him to." The slight curve of her lips said he would go to please her, not because of any attractions of Jeannie's.

As she thought of being alone on the boat with Tom she experienced an odd sinking feeling. She could still call off the sail, she knew, on some pretext or other. But she didn't. She turned from Betty with the fateful sense that the die had been cast. She and Tom would go out alone together, probably for the last time ever.

141

"Whenever he's ready, then," she threw over her shoulder, "we can leave."

To Betty's relief Tom needed no urging to go without her. Had it not been for her imperative need to get him out of the way she would have been furious at the alacrity with which he accepted the change in plans.

"I don't believe you were very enthusiastic even to begin with, were you?" He smiled down at her as she lay stretched out on the chaise longue in their room.

"I can't say I was. It doesn't sound much fun, sprawled all over the gunwales or whatever they are, soaked with spray and tangled up in a mess of rigging."

"You're not supposed to be tangled in the rigging; that's not the idea."

"*I* would be. Well, you run along with your little outdoor girl and don't worry about me. I trust you keep busy enough with the ropes and the steering to keep out of trouble."

"Right you are." Although he leaned over to kiss her good-by she had a definite impression of perfunctoriness in the gesture. Her resentment flared to useless rage as he flashed a brilliant smile from the door and exited into the hall. He couldn't wait to go off with the sweet girl graduate. Betty could see her gazing soulfully at him with those big cornflower eyes as they flew over the water, see their hands meeting and clinging on the ropes as they worked the sails. Damn!

A feeling of infinite depression settled on her as she

lay there with her eyes closed. Not only was Tom getting away from her, but she didn't even want him anymore. Except that she had no choice. To think of all the trouble to which she had gone to shed Al and her old life—not to mention the baby, of whom indeed she seldom thought nowadays, and then to find the new life so disappointing.

Tom had seemed a perfect catch. She had studied with great care the prospects open to her before settling on him. At least it was true that he made a whopping big salary; but after a few months with the greater affluence things had gotten very dull. Tom was really a clod, not too different from Al, just more money. It had taken the brush with the Judges to bring home to her the extent of her dissatisfaction. If she could only be Karen Judge. Or, rather, if she could be in Karen Judge's place. *That* was the way to live. And Harry. She hadn't yet sorted out how she felt about Harry. She did know he excited her. He was still good looking, even with the little bit of fat around his face—most of the effect of the added fat was to make him look more mature. The boyish look that had still characterized his features three years ago was gone, replaced with a quality she found hard to classify. There was something reckless about Harry, dangerous—a thirst for life which was that of a vital, sophisticated individual. His tastes and appetites were of a sort not satisfied in the course of ordinary living. Betty's eyes were open now and she studied the ceiling as if she were reading on it a description of the character of Harry Judge. Harry wanted life the way *she* wanted life: he wanted to devour it whole, in gulps. And not just any life: a life of excitement, of dangerous enthrallment, of shattering climaxes. The thought of his hands on her as they had been last night put her almost into a trance of desire.

She shivered and her fingers went up to her burning cheeks. God, Tom had never affected her like this. Then the memory of Harry crushing her hand as he said goodnight jerked her out of her reverie. Harry was a devil. She must keep her eyes on the cruel, evil side of him and not let herself be swept away. It was precisely this evil part which held her enthralled, or so she guessed. And because of it she must never let him gain ascendancy over her or she would be lost; he would kick her senseless and then trample what was left.

Harry is a murderer, she said to herself, a murderer. He has killed a man. A murderer. But repetition of the words did nothing to loosen his hold on her. Again she felt his hands, the touch of his lips. Actually, why shouldn't Harry have killed the old man? He hadn't much time left to him anyway, and meanwhile Harry would have been deprived of everything that was his right during the years it meant most to him.

She didn't blame him; she could be as ruthless herself about overcoming obstacles in her way. But she must make certain, when he came, that he recognized this—that they were cut from the same pattern. Then he'd know she was no bootlicker.

A knock at the door startled her so that she sat bolt upright, her nerves jangling like a set of wind chimes. It was Marcia, dressed for church, carrying a straw bag and white gloves, and with a small flowered hat on her head.

"We're just going. Can I do anything for you?"

"Oh, thanks, no. I'm fine."

"Feeling better?"

"Yes, I think so."

"You're sure you don't mind everyone's going off and leaving you? Jim could take the children to Sunday school and I could keep you company."

"Thanks, you're very sweet, but that's not necessary. I may just take a nap."

"Well, if you're sure. We'll be back from church a little after twelve." She waved and closed the door, calling, "Tim? We're going; go on down and get in the station wagon." Then as Marcia's steps receded down the hall, her voice from farther away, "Suzie?"

With eyes closed Betty listened to the backing out of the car, the babble of voices, the irritating shrillness of the children's predominating, as the sounds rose to the windows from the parking strip; she could visualize them all getting into the station wagon. The doors slammed shut and silence returned with their final departure.

In sudden alarm she peered at her watch. Ten-thirty. She got up and went to the dressing table to redo her lipstick and comb her hair. Would this dress do? Yes, it would have to; they'd think it strange if they came back from church and found her all dressed up in something different.

Eleven o'clock, he'd said. He was still coming, of course. The last thing he'd said had been the whispered reminder that he'd see her today. Well, she was ready for him. But she was surprised to find that her hands were shaking as she smoothed down her dress.

They were well out in the Sound now, beating to windward. There was quite a stiff breeze. Jeannie was helmsman, and already Tom had had ample opportunity to approve her seamanship. He could see that she had spent a lot of time on the water since he had given her those early lessons. Conversation was desultory, as they were both absorbed in the business of sailing. Tom sat out, balancing the boat on the weather side as it heeled in the wind. It was a fine feeling, with the green water rushing beneath him, creaming in the wake of the boat, and overhead the sails spread against the summer sky. Gulls wheeled and dipped. Their poignant cries, punctuating the restless quiet which hung over the water, brought back to Tom as could nothing else the feel and smell of boyhood summers on the Chesapeake Shore. The boat seemed a live thing, bearing them over the waves to the horizon. It was another life from the one that held him bound on shore. The sound of the water against the hull and the feel of the salt spray on his face made him mindlessly happy.

This was a much better boat than the second-hand dinghy Jim had first bought her.

"A good name for her—*Rover*." Tom looked up at the mast and ahead at the waves as they nosed into them. "Smacks of the seven seas. It could cause a good case of wanderlust."

"It's a double name. There's that—roving. But I always thought Rover was such a fine, old-fashioned and forthright name for a dog. Somehow it implies loyalty. I think of the boat like that—faithful, and a very personal thing, like a good dog."

She was right, he decided; when you thought of the boat that way it did seem more personal. Jeannie had always had odd little quirks, nice quirks, he realized, in the way she felt about things.

Land seemed far away now, even the near shore they had left. It huddled anonymously, dark green and formless, its people and their houses reduced almost to hypothetical existence. Shorebound problems were erased, leaving no mark.

"It's almost as if the last five years had never been," he said.

"Yes." Her eyes rested on him for a moment and then returned to the sail.

"As if it were just yesterday that we were sailing together like this. Only of course you've changed . . ."

Her eyes crinkled at the corners and narrowed between their long lashes. "Well, I hope I'm a better sailor; if I'm not there's no excuse."

"Oh, *that*. You're a whiz." They both knew he hadn't been referring to her ability to hoist a sail or keep it trimmed.

There were a tremendous number of boats out today—the sailboats, silent and sedate, dipping and bowing serenely across the water, the more aggressive motor craft cutting curly white wakes into the surface of the sea.

He tried to give some further thought to Betty and the probability of her being pregnant. She had seemed pretty sure this morning: morning sickness, she said she had, which made it look as if she were right. He concentrated for a few minutes on Betty as a mother, but the picture wouldn't come clear. He couldn't see her hovering over a crib. He had a distinct impression, though he could not say how he had picked it up—perhaps it was cumulative, from little things—that she didn't like children, particularly babies. Maybe she'd change with her own? He didn't feel very hopeful of it; in fact he had an uncomfortable feeling of apprehension on behalf of the life it seemed Betty was going to bring forth. He and the kid would have to stick together.

Somehow he found himself remembering Jeannie as she had looked yesterday, taking off for the beach with Tim and Suzie, laughing with them, happy in their company. Well, today was his day with her, and he mustn't spoil it with thoughts of other things.

"I don't know about you, but I'm starving," he informed her. They'd been out for more than an hour.

"Then we'll eat. It's not eleven yet, but I'm always hungry. I was going to put in at that little place—you know? where we used to go. But we don't have to. We can eat right out here."

"No, I like your choice. Let's head in."

It was still well before noon when they dropped anchor in the quiet cove. They had come here often before; it was a handy spot not too far up the coast from Henning where Jeannie had always kept her boat. They had gone swimming a couple of times off the dinghy, he remembered, when he had been teaching her how to sail it.

Now she brought out sandwiches and a thermos of coffee. Sitting next to him in the cockpit, she asked him more about his job in the New York office. They had touched on it Friday, in a polite and superficial way, when Betty had stood with them, the three of them talking. Now he realized from what she said that Jeannie had followed his progress closely in the years he'd been away; she was surprisingly familiar with some of the details of his life in Chicago. She must have badgered Jim about him. To know this for some reason filled him with a savage bitterness, a bitterness edged with guilt. There he had been in Chicago not even thinking about her, and she had been asking about him, caring what happened to him, feeling happy for him when he did well. But then why would he have thought of her, other than to smile and feel it would be pleasant to tweak her ponytail and tease her about something so that she would give out with that infectious laugh? After all, at twenty-six one didn't go about yearning over a girl of fifteen. Not if you were right in the head. Even now, thinking back to their times here in the cove, he could not invest his memories with even a shred of romance; she was still a stringy kid for whom he had felt a brotherly affection. The suddenness with which his feelings had changed still seemed little short of unbelievable. Had her feelings changed for him? She had probably, in that time he was remembering, when she was newly orphaned, put him in a class with the father she had lost: a kind adult on whom she could depend. So just remember that, old man, and don't be so touched that she thought of you while you were in Chicago; she's a thoughtful kid.

They had reached the cookies.

"What are you going to do when your day camp folds up at the end of the summer, look for another job?"

"I have one. Sort of assistant and secretary to the dean of women at K. U."

"Oh, I didn't know. Sounds good." He'd be able to visualize her then, when he no longer saw her in the fall. He could think of her crossing the campus—his campus and hers, it was—with the bright autumn colors over her head, see her pause on the steps of the old brick Ad. Building.

"I didn't know you could do secretarial stuff. Shorthand and everything?"

"Yes, I've taken a course the last two summers. I love the shorthand. Reading it back is like trying to decipher the Rosetta Stone, and then when you have, it seems miraculous: all those squiggles really mean something."

Tom grinned. "You're lost if you can't read it later, I know that. My new secretary in New York is completely mystified by her own notes; it means nothing to her after she's got it down."

Jeannie made a face. "I hope I won't have that trouble. It's marvelously fun to do, you know—positively sinister, like spy codes. The average person can't read shorthand at all."

"I'll have to ask my secretary if she feels sinister."

As Jeannie got up and moved past him to stow the remains of lunch she stumbled, and quickly Tom caught her hand to steady her. The feel of her slender fingers in his seemed stronger, suddenly, than any resolution he had made. He couldn't let go. He felt himself weakening and there was nothing but her face before him, the water around them and the sun beating down on them both, its heat drawing from him any resistance he had left. Sharply he took hold of himself, but already she had withdrawn her hand. Her eyes were lowered as they prepared to up anchor and get under way again, so that he was unable to see whether or not they held a reproach. A moment ago they had gazed at him, startled, as she felt the current that flowed from his fingers into hers. She couldn't have mistaken it, or the emotion in his face. You bastard! he said to himself. How could he think for a moment of involving her, trying to drag her down into a romance with a married man?

"Betty was a secretary, wasn't she?" Although she took up the conversation right where they had left off, the substance of it now was that of a stinging rebuke. If he hadn't the decency to keep his wife in mind, she would do it for him.

"Yes." He almost bit off the word.

"Was that how you met her? Was she your secretary?"

"Yes, that's how I met her. But she was someone else's. Someone else's secretary, I mean. Next office."

"I see." Her voice was toneless, withdrawn, and he wondered what she was thinking. The mood of joy which had sent them scudding across the water this morning as though running before the wind had been broken: it was like a jibe all standing, when suddenly the wind blew from another quarter, smashing the boom over without warning and bringing them up shaken and damaged.

Silent now, wary, and distrustful of themselves, they pulled the anchor up and got under way. Tom took the helm. As they came out of the shelter of the cove it was immediately evident that the wind was much stronger than before.

With one last backward look at the cove, Jeannie said, "We'd better head for home, don't you think?"

"If you say so."

"Well, hadn't we? Since Betty couldn't come—"

"Yes. Yes, of course we should go back," he said heavily.

They stayed closer to shore this time, sailing before the wind, which had changed direction a little now and had indeed gained in force. They fairly flew along. Tom stared stonily out to sea, painfully aware of Jeannie close beside him and savagely telling himself he mustn't touch her again, no matter how much he wanted to.

But in spite of the blackness of his mood, gradually the healing air of the sea washing over him brought back a semblance of the happiness that always went with a day of sailing. It was impossible to be out there with the green water under him and the sails taut in the wind and not feel that just being alive was a gift beyond price. There was a healing quality, too, in the look of Jeannie, her brown young form and the lovely face with the intensely blue eyes that put the sea to shame. He found himself turning repeatedly to look at her, as he kept a lookout for other boats, and discovered that she did not flinch away but gazed back at him— somehow, he felt, bemused. The feeling of tension between them ebbed away.

They had both been watching the approach from far ahead and somewhat to the left of a good-sized motor yacht, coming toward them on a parallel course at what looked like top speed. From behind, also to the left, they were being overtaken by an Atlantic class sloop.

"Isn't she lovely?" Jeannie turned to admire the larger "A" boat as its sleek black hull, cutting the water effortlessly, came abreast of them and slowly drew ahead. It was a beautiful sight, its sails billowed out in the wind.

Tom, returning his attention to their own sails, frowned as he saw that the jib was not drawing properly. Jeannie, alert it seemed to every lift of his eyebrow, glanced up and saw, too, that it hung slack and useless, blanketed by the mainsail.

"We'll try wing and wing," he said. This meant spreading the jib to starboard, since the boom was out on the port side, and they would then be sailing "wung-out," flying along like a bird with a wing to each side.

But the jib sheet was stuck. He couldn't get it to move.

"I'll see what's wrong." Jeannie slid from his side and went forward.

The sloop to port had drawn ahead of them now, eclipsing for a few moments the motor yacht which was nearing it from ahead on the "A" boat's left. Then as the black hull slid ahead, the power boat, about a forty-five footer as Tom could see now, cut astern of her on a new course and headed straight for the spot where the *Rover* would be in a couple of minutes.

"Tom—" Jeannie called in alarm from up forward, where she had just succeeded in freeing the jib sheet.

"Yes. What the hell does he think he's doing?" From a parallel course the craft had veered to what looked like a collision course. Probably the skipper, busy watching the "A" boat, had misjudged the speed or position of the *Rover;* now he would have to alter course immediately. The rules of the road were clear enough: a power boat must give way to sail.

Tom had never been one to insist pigheadedly on the right-of-way just because it was his; no sailor with any sense did that. But in this case there wasn't much he could do; in fact any change he could make in course might only worsen things.

And now there was almost no time at all. Whoever was at the wheel of the craft bearing down on them must, Tom concluded, be a rank amateur; either he mistakenly believed he would make it across Tom's bow, or he expected the sailboat to give way. Just because the *Rover* was smaller, did he think his big expensive power job deserved the privilege of staying on course?

Tom could not have altered course before for fear the other boat would do so at the same time, that being its duty. But now he must. He felt his innards tighten as he gathered himself together for action. He looked worriedly forward at Jeannie, perched by the jib.

"Hang on! We're going to have to jibe!" He heard his own voice as he prepared to put the helm over, knowing what would happen.

"Oh, no!" cried Jeannie, looking anxiously aloft, afraid the mast would snap, love for her boat stronger than fear for her own safety.

The wind had been dead astern, but as the bow turned to port in response to the rudder change, the wind, perilously strong under the circumstances, would get on the wrong side of the sail and slam the boom over, a killing blow for anyone in its way.

Tom prayed that Jeannie would hang on tight. Then two things happened: he put the helm over, felt the boat's response as she swung to the left; and he looked up, too late, to see that Jeannie was climbing back towards the cockpit, into the path where the boom would swing over. She must have thought she'd have time to make it before he changed course.

"Get forward! Jeannie!" he called, agonizingly conscious of the narrow space by which the *Rover*'s boom cleared the deck. But there was no time for her to get back to a position of safety, he knew that.

He was aware of the tiller under his hand, the main sheet between his fingers, and of the sleek white prow of their adversary, the big yacht, plowing towards them with all the lethal power of a killer shark; and of the slender figure clinging to a precarious handhold just forward of the cockpit.

The boom whipped over his head, tearing the main sheet from his hand. He felt rather than saw Jeannie go over the side, and in that moment the world turned cruel and lonely. He didn't know whether the boom had struck her, but the enormity of the thought somehow made it at once a dread certainty in his mind. Dimly he was conscious of the yacht going safely past him and away, leaving him lurching in its wake with a cold sickness at the pit of his stomach. Frantically his eyes searched the rolling waters behind him.

At last he had hold of her and his big, strong hands reached down for her and he pulled her aboard. It had seemed an eternity before he had caught sight of her, a small wet head bobbing in the wake of the boat, and another eternity before he could come about and pick her up.

"Damn his soul!" He cursed the road hog who had continued on his way with obviously no concern about picking up survivors.

"Are you all right?" He pulled her down in the cock-pit beside him.

"Yes. I slipped, that's all."

She was all right. That was the only thing that mattered and the fact erased for him the memory of any other moment than this. She was close against him, safe under his hands, for he held her now by the shoulders. Her shirt and shorts were plastered to her, the streaked light hair hung darkened and sodden on her neck.

And without even thinking about it, except to feel that this was inevitable, he kissed her as he had been wanting to. Her lips were cold from the sea water. The coldness of death, it could have been; the reminder brought his arms around her till he held her close.

His head came up almost with a snap as the realization swept over him that he couldn't do this.

He looked long at her, this lovely creature, the girl he should have waited for.

"I'm sorry," he whispered. She gazed at him like one bewitched. "I'd no right to do that; none in the world."

She made no answer. He didn't know it, but he was seeing on her face the same lost look that had so upset Quint the night before when they'd been talking of Tom. His conscience closed in on him with sharp finality. He must put the lid on this.

With an effort he smiled, and with an attempt at humor which he feared fell short by miles, said, "Chalk up another conquest, my dear, to those beautiful blue eyes." The eyes flickered and her face stiffened warily. For an instant the hurt showed, and then her guard was up.

Fortunately he had the boat to get under way again. Miraculously there had been no damage as a result of the accidental jibe. Woodenly Jeannie remarked as much and without need of instruction took up her crewing chores again.

Had Tom but known it, her world lay in ruins. That one moment had been everything—stolen, of course, because it should never have been, but twice as sweet for that bitterness. And then in the next breath he had destroyed everything that lay between them. He thought she was a cheap flirt and he was, it seemed, just playing along.

She glanced over at him and caught him gazing grimly at her, his face unexpectedly haggard. She hoisted her chin in the air and gave her attention back to the way ahead, dotted to the horizon with small white sails. She had her pride, at least.

"How do you like the *Rover,* now that you've sailed her?" she threw over her shoulder.

"Great. She's really a good boat."

There the conversation died.

Presently she caught him watching her, the tenderness and affection there for her to see because he couldn't hide them. He hadn't, then, meant it the way it had sounded—what he'd said.

She had to know.

"You didn't actually think I—that I've been flirting with you, as an amusement or something?" She felt the color burning in her face.

He shook his head. "You didn't really need to ask that, did you?" He touched her gently on the cheek. After a little he went on in a voice ragged with emotion. "You see, I didn't know. My God, you were only fifteen when I left. I never dreamed—"

There was nothing for her to say, she could only look at him.

Today Marcia wasn't even trying to follow the sermon. Not that she usually did, except for scraps here and there. Always she came away feeling renewed and restored to harmony with the world, and with the conviction that she had been spiritually uplifted by some process similar to osmosis, in which goodness and mercy and all those other qualities so highly thought of in the Bible had seeped through from the atmosphere about her and improved in some measure her inner condition. But this morning she drew no comfort from the phrases of the sermon as they passed over her head into oblivion, nor did the hymns bind up her wounds and succor her as they said they would. The only words she seemed to pick out of the air were those applying to the nether world. Woe everlasting flowed down the aisle of the church and lapped at the steps to the pulpit. Dr. Gibney couldn't help her.

She kept thinking of Jim's phone conversation with Quint this morning. She had stood in the doorway to the den watching him, his face grave as he sat on the edge of the desk, doodling like mad on the phone pad as he talked, and trying, she could tell, to make light of something—probably for her benefit since he knew she was listening. She had gone over to see what he was writing on the pad, but there were only patterns and nervous scribbles, no words.

"What is it?" she asked when he at last hung up.

"Quint's been talking to Fellini this morning. Seems they haven't found any acquaintances of Mrs. Wiebald's who might have wanted to do her in. And since they've now double-checked and established the fact that she had never sat for any of the people attending our party that night, attention is focusing on me again, as owner and driver of the car, and employer of Mrs. Wiebald."

"Oh, Jim! That's not fair!"

He shrugged hopelessly. "Well, what else have they got to go on? Quint says Captain Fellini may ask me if I'll consent to take a lie-detector test."

"Oh." She had frowned. "And what did you say?"

"I said I would."

But would that clear him? She wondered about that now. She was sure the police as yet knew nothing about

161

Jim's blackouts. But if they found out, would a lie-detector test do anything to prove his innocence? Captain Fellini might decide that a clean bill of health from their little machine meant nothing, because he could still have killed Mrs. Wiebald and not, himself, be aware of it.

Awful as it was having the police suspect Jim, what to Marcia seemed even worse was Jim's own feeling about the case. If only he could shake off this doubt of himself, this fear of what he might have done in those forgotten hours. Marcia herself was sure. For her the one incontrovertible fact was that someone *other* than Jim had killed poor Mrs. Wiebald and was now standing aside letting Jim take the blame. This person cast a shadow, she knew, as surely as if he were standing there watching them. For she felt the shadow, like an evil thing; it had fallen on her blotting out the light, and from that darkness she could not see whose shadow it was.

"I think you've had what you came for—by now," Betty had said wisely, pushing Harry away.

The desk clock in the den showed eleven-thirty and the Townsends weren't due back from church for three-quarters of an hour or more, but she wanted him out of here with time to spare.

"Not quite." There was something faintly chilling in his tone. Oh, no, she thought.

"You're a very attractive little piece, of course." His voice was like metal, slick and hard. "But I can't really trust you—can I."

"Listen." She put her arms around him again, her face close to his as they sat on the long leather couch. "You *know* you can trust me. Haven't I proved—"

"Lovers can fall out, my dear."

"Not in this case, Harry darling, because we're alike. I never knew I was like that till I met you, and we—hit it off. Laugh if you will, but till you started in on me I really thought I was quite a nice girl. Just misunderstood."

He cocked an eyebrow at her. "You're not going to top all this by trying to tell me I *seduced* you?"

"Hardly. I've taken up with you with my eyes wide open. And it hasn't been because you threatened me; that only added to the thrill." Her voice turned husky, with a sensuous quality the like of which Harry had encountered nowhere else. "Harry! You're a man as no one I've ever met before has been."

Already, he knew, he had waited too long. For one last time he allowed himself to wish that he could have this girl instead of Karen. It wasn't possible: the money was Karen's, and the stock in the company belonged to Karen, her aunt, and her cousins, *et cetera, et cetera.* He was Karen's family's paid employee.

Harry put aside the useless wishes. With a touch of

163

scorn he noticed how her hair was coming in dark at the roots. She was just a cheap little bauble, after all.

"You're not afraid of me?"

"No." She looked at him unflinchingly.

"When you are pretty sure I'm a murderer?"

She didn't bat an eyelash. "That's nothing to do with me."

He smiled. "Ah, you trust me. You really do."

"I said so."

"And I'll trust you, once you've done one little thing for me."

"What is it?"

He crossed to the desk and motioned to the chair. "Sit down."

Hesitantly she did as he asked.

"All I want is a simple document in your handwriting, which I shall keep, guaranteeing, I can assure you, that you will not want to squeal on me—should our loving pact ever wear thin."

"Do you really think that's necessary?" Actually she was relieved. Was this to be all?

"Very necessary."

"You're putting an unwanted strain on our 'loving pact,' you know."

"I can't help that. I'd rather be sure first and enjoy myself afterwards."

"Sounds like you. You're wrong, of course." She opened the top drawer and brought out a writing pad.

An automatic pencil lay on the leather-framed blotter. "What kind of document?"

"I'll dictate. 'I am not really Betty Graham. My name is Elizabeth Melinder and I am still the legal wife of Albert Melinder of Cressland. Mrs. Wiebald knew. That's why I had to kill her. I—' "

She stopped writing abruptly. "*Kill* her!" She stared up at him dumfounded. "I'm not going to write that! I *didn't*—"

He cut in. "I know you didn't kill her." He spoke with a patience that was deliberate, patience that was fury barely restrained. "But what better insurance could I have of your continued loyalty and cooperation than to keep this signed 'confession'—"

"But when I didn't *do* it! You have enough on me without that: bigamy. I'd lose Tom, everything, and you don't even need a signed paper. A telephone call to Al would do well enough. So why this, confessing to a murder?"

His glance went to the desk clock. Too much time was passing. "Because your marriage, your fortune, isn't your life. You've got to have as much risk in this liaison as I have, or it's no dice."

"No dice? Describe that part of it to me," she said coldly.

"Easy. I'll show you." He had been standing just behind her, looking over her shoulder as she wrote. To talk to him she had half turned in the chair. Now he moved to the wall just beside him, keeping an eye on her. There was a wall safe let into the paneling. It was unlocked, for he opened it at once without twirling the knob. But the safe scarcely garnered her notice. What riveted her attention on Harry while waves of sick terror pulsed through her was the fact that he had put on gloves. He had taken them out and put them on while he had stood behind her chair.

He caught her fascinated gaze and an ugly smile spread across his face showing his small, even teeth, somewhat pointed like a piranha's. "Yes, gloves, dear, like in Perry Mason. Just in case it becomes necessary. That's what you want to know about, isn't it—the 'or else'?" From the safe he took a revolver and inspected it. "Jim always keeps this here. Loaded."

"Well, don't point it at me. I don't like guns."

"Then you see why you're to finish the document. Without it you and I have no future at all. You in particular."

She tried a plea straight from the heart. She loved him. Wasn't that enough?

"No."

"Mrs. Wiebald knew," she wrote, as he had dictated.

" 'That's why I had to kill her. I can't go on with it,' " Harry continued.

And she stopped writing. That last sentence was the tip-off: this was not a confession Harry was going to keep, this was a suicide note.

"Why do I write that?" she asked sharply.

"Because I say so."

Still her pencil did not move on the pad. She cocked her head. "I hear someone. Don't you?"

Harry turned to listen. Silently he crossed to the hall door, watching her sidelong. He didn't see the stealthy movement of her hand to the telephone pad, nor guess at the tiny cryptic message she was able to put there among the doodles on the paper. It was in shorthand, just squiggles and a line among the curlicues Jim had traced there that morning: *Harry Judge killed*

It was all she had time for. She hoped someone would get the message, because she didn't want him to get away with it. She knew now what was going to happen to her. She knew, too, what she should have sensed before: the violent death beneath the Jaguar, which she had watched from the safety of the trees, was meant to have been hers.

Her last thought, strangely enough, was of her mother—almost like a silent prayer it was, the thought that went with the picture of the slightly plump, smooth, kind face. If you were only here, Mom, to help me! Dear Mother! You wouldn't like it, what's happening to your girl. If you were only here to help your Liz this . . .

It was Jim who found her when they came home from church, luckily not one of the children or Marcia.

167

For the second time in forty-eight hours he was looking at death, and it was no less grotesque or horrible than the first time. For the second time he gazed down in pity mingled still with unbelief at what had been so short a time ago a living, breathing human being, now strangely transmogrified. She was sprawled forward in the desk chair, her head resting on the blotter which was crimsoned at the edge of her hair with a soaked-up puddle of blood. The gun was still clutched in her hand.

For one horrified moment the thought crossed his mind, oh, no, will I be blamed for this one, too? And then he remembered with a wave of thankfulness that he had been in church. Dozens of people could testify that he couldn't have been here when it happened. His eye fell on the penciled note lying beside the still, blonde head. Fascinated, he read to the end:

I am not really Betty Graham. My name is Elizabeth Melinder and I am still the legal wife of Albert Melinder of Cressland. Mrs. Wiebald knew. I can't

She hadn't finished. And there was no signature.

He touched nothing, except to take the key from the inside of the door and transfer it to the outside of the lock. He closed the door behind him and turning the key, pocketed it and walked down the hall in search of Marcia.

Almost as unexpected as the girl's death was the astonishing contents of the suicide note. Not really married to Tom, after all. He could hardly take it in. And that about Mrs. Wiebald?

He found Marcia in the kitchen, rummaging in the refrigerator.

"Where are the children?" he asked hollowly.

At the odd sound of his voice she closed the refrigerator door and slowly turned. Something was very wrong. "Why, they've gone upstairs to change from their Sunday best."

"You'd better get them out of here, take them someplace. Betty's shot herself. She's in the den."

Marcia drew a long, deep breath and asked, "Is she dead?"

"Quite." He took down the yellow kitchen wallphone and dialed the number for the police.

"*Poor Tom,*" she said, very low, as Jim replaced the phone.

"They'll be right out—naturally. Yes, poor Tom. And that's not all. She's left a note. She wasn't even married to Tom; she's a bigamist. Was."

"She—*what?*"

"She's still married to her first husband, someone living in Cressland."

"Oh, *poor* Tom!" At the same time she was glad he was rid of her. Not in this dreadful way, of course, but his taking up with her at all had been a terrible mistake —even more of a mistake, it now seemed, than anyone could have guessed.

"And one ironical piece of good news: it may be that I'm cleared of suspicion in Mrs. Wiebald's death. Betty says something about her in the note."

"Oh, Jim!" She hugged him hard, her face for an instant radiant. "But good heavens, about Tom. Even worse, isn't it! Someone's got to break it to him, Jim; he can't just get back from sailing and run smack into the police, and the ambulance parked in the drive and all. I'll go, and wait for them to come in."

"What are you going to do with Tim and Suzie?"

"I'll drop them at Karen's; it's right on the way to the yacht club."

And so it was that when Jeannie and Tom had tied up the *Rover* at her mooring and come ashore Marcia was waiting for them, sitting in her station wagon in the parking lot. Side by side, saying nothing to each other, they walked to Tom's car. They hadn't seen her waiting for them; they were not expecting her. Marcia had opened the car door and started to get out when she was suddenly struck by the odd way the two of them were standing by Tom's convertible. Jeannie made no move to get in, nor did he open the door for her. They just stood there wordlessly, looking at each other. Abruptly Marcia sat down again.

So that was the way it was. And she was remembering Jeannie at fourteen, dark circles under her eyes, a fragile, lonesome-looking child, brightening to an unexpected appearance of health when Tom Graham came out unannounced for the weekend; she attached herself to him like a stray dog to a newfound master every time he came. And Jeannie at fifteen, taller and older, and starting to be a little pretty, her ponytail bobbing as she bounced into the house saying, "Tom's really coming, isn't he?" She and Jim had both thanked God for Tom, he had been such a help getting their orphaned charge over the difficult time and established in a new place. Jeannie had even said once to Marcia, "I'm going to marry Tom when I'm older; there couldn't be anyone else for me, ever." And it had been a perfectly usual schoolgirl crush; such attachments were the norm at fourteen or so, when boys the same age were still so callow and hopeless. But all that should have been water over the dam for Jeannie long ago. She hadn't even seen Tom in years.

And that was just it, wasn't it? Jeannie had been no more prepared for a rekindling of her feelings for Tom than had Marcia for her awareness of it now. No wonder Jeannie had been so strange and withdrawn—and so downhearted, which was completely unlike her. It had puzzled Marcia, because she and her sister-in-law were like sisters, and Jeannie always confided in her. Not this time. Now Marcia could see why. This was not something she could talk about, and perhaps she had been trying to fight it off. From all appearances she had lost badly.

She wondered how Tom felt, and as she again opened

her door and getting out of the station wagon walked towards them, she could see well enough that their plight was mutual. He had it just as bad. And if she had wondered even for a moment how far things might have gone, she could see in the defeated look of both of them that they were making an end of the whole thing as they stood there on the hot asphalt of the yacht club parking lot.

Well, surely now things would straighten out. Tom was free after all.

"Tom—" she called.

They both looked up as she crossed the asphalt to the car.

Chapter 7

SUCH an old cliché that one is: the murderer always re-
turns to the scene of his crime. So far as anyone knew
there was no murderer anyway; it had been a suicide.
Only Quint suspected that she hadn't killed herself, and
he had said nothing to anyone of his doubts. So when
Jeannie left the day camp on Tuesday afternoon she
did not guess that her path and Harry's would cross.

She could have stayed home yesterday and today, certainly, skipping her counselor duties, but what good
would that have done anyone? It was better to get out
in the sun and keep frantically busy all day, busy
enough that she wouldn't have a moment to think. It
was better to be out of Tom's way, too.

From the moment Marcia had told him on Sunday,
Tom had become a total stranger, drawn into himself
and looking at her as if she didn't exist. He had been
closeted for what seemed hours Sunday night with Jim,

173

and since then had talked in subdued fashion with Jim or with Marcia, and with Quint, too, for he had come over both evenings. But from Jeannie he drew away, answering her only in monosyllables, turning cold, his manner almost cutting.

She was afraid she knew why. Granted Betty was in the wrong about everything (imagine marrying Tom when she was already married! And imagine, too, her walking out on her husband and baby in the first place), still Tom could be blaming himself for causing her to take her own life. Up till now Betty had lived with what she had done. But if now she had thought she was losing Tom to Jeannie, mightn't her life suddenly have become unbearable, not worth the candle? Thus Tom's thoughts might be running, so that he hated himself, Jeannie, and the tie they had both discovered that bound them together. For once he had loved Betty; he must have, to marry her. And now she was dead— through his fault and hers?

And was Betty a murderer as well? Jeannie was by no means sure of that. The note hadn't actually said so. What Tom himself believed on the subject she couldn't even guess.

As she drove towards home in the little Volkswagen she saw nothing of the roadway or the intersections she passed or the traffic through which she threaded her way. She thought of those moments on board the *Rover*, those precious moments when she had felt his lips on hers and had known with a singing certainty that he loved her, wrong or right. Now the memory was fixed for her in the past tense and with crystal clarity, kept timelessly like one of those ocean-bottom scenes in the clear paperweights—the dead sea horse and the examples of marine flora and a shell, imprisoned forever in pellucid plastic.

No one was home when she reached the house. Marcia must either have gone shopping or taken the children swimming. Tom could be anywhere; he was staying on with them, of course. His aunt was coming from Baltimore this evening and would be staying with them too. Come to think of it, Marcia must have taken the children over to the Carraways', where they would be till after Betty's funeral, partly because Aunt Francie would have Tim's room. The Carraways had seven children, amongst whom, according to Mrs. Carraway, two more wouldn't even be noticed.

She went into the den to look at the mail. She disliked going in there now, because of what had happened, but she might as well get used to it. She bent over the desk, now devoid of the ill-fated leather-framed blotter. There was a letter from her best friend from K. U., Toinette. Unable to bring herself to sit down in the desk chair to read it, she slit it open with the silver paper knife and read it standing up. Toinette was engaged. How nice. She smiled as she put the letter back in the blue-lined envelope. Then it was that her eye lighted on the phone pad, covered with Jim's doodles. But not only with Jim's doodles.

At first she thought she was having hallucinations. It was too much of a coincidence. It had been only day before yesterday that she had laughingly told Tom how much fun she found shorthand because it was like code. "The average person can't read shorthand at all." Her own words came back to her. And Betty must have banked on that, must have been quite sure that the person she named in her note wouldn't even guess that his name was written there for someone else to see.

"Harry Judge killed—"

It could mean nothing else. Betty had written it. She had had no time to write more before he killed her. Killed her, and had killed Mrs. Wiebald? Was that what the message meant?

Karen flashed across her mind. Good God! Karen had been living with a murderer? Alarm and anger caught her up. The outrageousness of it!

Opening the desk drawer she took out the phone book and with shaking fingers searched through its pages for the number of Quint's law firm. Quint would know what to do, she would call him at once.

Doubting, and doubting again, Karen had come to see Quint at his office in Cressland.

"Why, yes, Mrs. Judge. He's in," said Marge, his secretary.

And then she was sitting in the comfortable leather chair across the desk from Quint. Now that she was here, she didn't know what to say.

"Quint, I need your help . . . you offered it . . ."

"Of course." The office seemed at once homey, with Karen sitting there, her eyes limned by the dark smudges under them. There was an odd blue mark along the line of her jaw. Could Harry have struck her? "Anything I can do, Karen; you know that."

"Yes." Abruptly her eyes met his, and he saw fear in them. "I want to leave him, Quint. I want a divorce. Finally."

He got up and came around the desk. Drawing up another chair, he sat down beside her and took her hand. With a hard grip she squeezed his fingers, held on. "You'll know what to do. You see . . . I'm afraid. If I ask him for a divorce I don't know what he'll do. He might even kill me, I don't know."

"What makes you think that?"

"Well, it's a terrible thing to say, but it may be so. The last few days he's been—different. One minute he's exhilarated, reckless, devil-may-care—and the devil may care for me, of course. You must know how he feels about me. And then he turns crafty, vicious, asking me all kinds of questions and throwing in little torments. Not that that's unusual, but it's become much worse. I almost think he's cracking up."

Quint's odd greenish eyes flickered; their tic seemed

more pronounced today. "When did he start acting so —differently?"

"Friday night, I think. After the Townsends' dinner party, when the sitter was killed. On the way home he seemed distinctly odd. And ever since. The night of our party he was—dreadful." She shivered.

"Um." He nodded, thinking. He was far from convinced that the Mrs. Wiebald business was all wrapped up. There was an implication in that note Betty Graham—correction, Liz Melinder—had left, and the police had been ready enough to take it up, luckily clearing Jim; an implication that Liz might have been responsible for Mrs. Wiebald's death. But her sentence had never been completed. She hadn't *said* she had done it. And to Quint the note sounded as if it had been dictated—by someone else. At gun's point? It didn't seem like a suicide note, for several reasons. One, it had not been addressed to anyone—such as "Dear Tom," the logical candidate. Two, it had not been finished. Usually the suicide, if he went to the trouble to write a note, wanted it made clear why he was doing this and would finish the note, once it was begun. In fact usually it was an outcry against someone else who had made this step irrevocable, someone who had grievously wronged the suiciding party; there was no such tone to Betty's letter.

So he pricked up his ears when Karen went on about Harry's strange behavior.

"And now," she finished, "I'm stopped. I haven't the

physical courage to tell him we're through. He'll be
. . . well, you know, Quint: he'll be frantic. The
money is mine, that's why he stays with me. The company, even, belongs to my family; once Harry and I are
divorced—well, you know Aunt Helen, and Mr. Wal-
den—Dad's best friend. They're not going to leave
Harry in there as head of the company; he's only had
the job because he was the nearest thing Dad had to a
son and heir. But this will finish him off with the Kendrick enterprises. You know as well as I do."

"Very true. He's not been too good as president anyhow, as I hear it."

"Quint, what will he do, do you think?"

"Well, it won't be pretty to see."

"No."

"I'll be with you when you tell him."

"Is that wise? He knows that you . . ."

"He knows I've just been waiting around, ever since
he cut me out. And I don't give a damn what he thinks
about it, one way or another." He took her other hand
as well and held them both. "How about you? It won't
upset you too much to have me do battle for you? After
all I'm your lawyer."

"No, it's all right. I depend on you so, Quint; I know
it will be all right if you're there."

"And afterward? After it's all over, I mean. How are
my chances, Karen? Not that I want to push you."

"Afterward?" She shook her head, almost dazedly.

"I'm not sure I'll ever feel anything for anyone again. I'm—it's as if I'd been anesthetized for years. I'm dead inside. But I hope I'll get over it."

He pressed her hands comfortingly. "You will."

"Well if you're still around when I rejoin the living, no one else but you could ever matter, Quint. I can tell you that much now."

For a minute he just sat with his eyes closed.

"You want to do this right away? Harry?"

"Yes."

"Then I'll call him at the office and arrange to talk."

But Harry wasn't there. He had left the office early and would not be back. Quint tried him at home with no luck either.

The look of strain had come back to Karen's face. "Then I'll go on home and say nothing to him yet."

"All right. I'll drop over this evening, unannounced . . . And meantime—don't cross him."

He hated to see her go. But at least she had decided.

She hadn't been gone more than twenty minutes when his phone rang.

"Quint, this is Jeannie." Her voice was odd, muffled with excitement. "I've just found something. Here in the study where Betty was killed."

"Was—killed, you said?"

"Yes. I don't think she shot herself at all, she was murdered. She left a message, and it must—"

She broke off. "Oh. It's you—" he heard her say before the phone went dead.

In ten seconds he was going down the steps of the second-floor office to the street—three at a time. Already in that time he had given the address to Marge, who would call the Rockton police. He would do his level best to get there. But he knew without the barest shadow of doubt that he would never be in time.

It had been Tom who made the funeral arrangements on Monday. The police quoted Albert Melinder, after they had talked to him about the tragedy when he came down to identify the body as that of his late—or as he put it, his "late, late"—wife, as saying, "She's all his now; let him bury her." This remark was also printed in the Cressland paper, which was black with headlines for once not about the tax rate or sewage contracts. Its front page was solid with pictures of everyone involved.

Tom still could not assimilate the fact that he had not been married. He had been so long held in the trap of marital discord that he still felt its jaws. It *had* been a marriage, for both of them—except for a small technicality. It had had the substance and texture of marriage, though not the quality, to take the word at its highest value.

And married or not, he still felt responsible for her.

On his part the whole thing had been begun in good faith, the promise of which he had patently not lived up to. The fact that she had felt driven to kill herself proved that he had failed her.

He was horrified by what she had done. The bigamy, that is—deserting her family and marrying him. He even wondered if it had been a case of amnesia—hit on the head in the train wreck and unable later to remember anything but her name. For the name she had gone by in her new life had been her own: Elizabeth Miller. She had switched from Liz to Betty, but then she mightn't have remembered what her nickname had been before the accident. The unloved childhood in the Bronx she could have made up and believed herself. Amnesiacs did that, he understood: reconstructed whole past histories for themselves.

The end result of his meditations was that he felt somehow dragged down and defiled by the whole train of events. Technically he was free now—had always been free, had he known it, to love Jeannie and to marry her. But morally this seemed impossible. He couldn't ask Jeannie to come to him, with the unsavory mess his life had turned out to be. Strangely, since the moment Marcia had told him the grisly tidings he had felt parted irrevocably from Jeannie, as though he had taken a turn carrying him away from her on another road. Even the tender, loving feeling he had had for her was gone, cauterized as by acid.

Well, she would forget him, and be better off when she did. And as for him—well, he didn't care what happened to him now. At least not at the present time, he didn't.

Had Betty killed that woman? He thought not. But even by that he felt soiled. The papers said she had. He didn't know.

Monday he had made the funeral arrangements— picked the casket and arranged for the service at the mortuary, with the minister from the church in Cressland which Betty's family had always attended. The service was to be Wednesday. Today he had a duty he dreaded even more. Betty's parents had, of course, been reached in Florida. They had flown up yesterday, and they wanted to see him, talk to him.

That was where he was going now, this afternoon. What made it even worse was that they were staying at Betty's house in Cressland. Albert Melinder's house. Mr. Miller, however, had assured him when they spoke on the phone that Al would not be there when he came.

This must be it, a large field full of nearly identical tri-levels painted different colors, some with brick trim, others with stone. The imposing sign at the brick-wall flanked gateway to the development said "Highland Estates." There were no highlands.

He found the street and pulled up in front of the neat yellow and white house that was 23 Apple Lane. An attractive, homey little place it was, with a yard full of flowers (not Betty's work, those), but definitely not the sort of establishment Betty would have wanted. He could imagine how it must have galled her to view the other houses of the same design, clearly lower-income dwellings, from her small front picture window, knowing that she was living in one just like them.

Mr. Miller, a small man with a full head of gray hair and a narrow, cheerful face, welcomed him into the house with a firm handshake.

"How are you, Mr. Graham? I'm Liz's father."

"How do you do, Mr. Miller. I'm so sorry—"

"Well, we all are. Even Al, though he won't admit it. Looks as if she picked herself a fine young man, didn't she, Mother?" He turned to the woman who sat on the Danish-type sofa with her arm around a small, blond boy. Mrs. Miller rose and crossed the room to extend him her hand. Considerably younger than her husband, she reminded Tom of the female half in those insurance adds of the couple saying "We retired to Florida in only fifteen years." She was the all-American mother, slightly plump in the face and comfortably proportioned farther down as well. She had been crying, a fact her black and silver pixie-tilted glasses failed to hide.

Tom's glance went past her to the child perched on the sofa, and at the instant recognition he experienced an odd contraction in the region of his chest. The boy was a small copy of Betty—blond hair, big brown eyes and all.

Mrs. Miller sat down again, her arm once more around her grandson. "This is Dickie."

"Yes, I can see." He hadn't meant it to sound so harsh, and added more gently, "He looks just like her."

"Doesn't he, though!" For a moment Betty's mother lit up, as she hugged her charge. Then the tears started oozing out again and she dabbed under her glasses with a damply balled handkerchief. "I just can't stop, I'm sorry!" she apologized.

"Dickie's Grandmother Melinder has been looking after him all this time, you know. But she's gone over to a friend's while we're here, so we'd have a place to stay. Motels are so expensive."

Didn't want to meet me, either, thought Tom thankfully.

"I just can't imagine how she could do it!" burst out Mrs. Miller at last, getting down finally to the subject. "Leave them." She nodded down at Dickie. "Of course she never killed that woman the way it said in the paper, I *know* that! You don't think she did—do you?"

"No, I can't believe she did."

"And they haven't proved it, have they? So I know she didn't. I've wondered, Mr. Graham—"

"Tom."

"Oh, thank you, Tom." Again the tears started, this time trickling down her cheeks before she blotted them off. "I've wondered about this other—the going off; clearly she did that. Could she have been out of her mind, something like that? She wasn't what I'd call a saint, but certainly she was a decent girl. And so happy she was when she married him. Al. And this little angel." She dropped a kiss on top of the blond head. "You'd know, she's been with you—how long was it?"

"Ten months."

"Ten months. Maybe you noticed, if she didn't seem quite right. I'd feel so much better if I thought she didn't do it on purpose, wasn't responsible, like." Tom tried to slip in an answer, but there was no stemming the tide of words. "She was a fine girl, you know, knew right from wrong. Never gave us any trouble, did she Dad?" Dad shook his head, experienced by now in not trying to compete verbally. "Tell me, Tom, do you think—?"

At last she had stopped.

Tom started carefully but kept going, trying to make sure she didn't interrupt him until he was finished. "She was perfectly sane, Mrs. Miller. Nothing crazy that I could see. But I've wondered myself if she mightn't have had amnesia after that train wreck."

"Amnesia." She considered it.

"I don't know what a doctor would say, or how long a thing like that lasts, but it seems to me it might have happened. A concussion suffered in the wreck, and she came out of it not knowing where she lived or remembering anything about her past life except her name."

"Why that could be, couldn't it? It could have happened that way. Do you think so, Dad?"

"Could be." Mr. Miller's tone implied that the whole thing was beyond him and his wife could pick any solution she liked.

"And then when it wore off and she remembered," she went on, "that could be why she . . . well, when she put an end to everything." She refrained from designating the end because as she would probably have said herself, Tom thought, little pitchers have big ears.

Tom left finally at about four-thirty, feeling that at least he had brightened their day a little. It had apparently meant a lot to them to talk to him. Such decent people, they were. So unlike Betty. That was an uncharitable thought, but why blink it? The doctor who had done the autopsy had told him that Betty could have had no reason to suspect that she was expecting a child. Tom had chewed at length on that piece of information, whatever it was worth.

He climbed into his car and drove slowly back to the Townsends', wishing to God he could get out of here. He was going to stay, of course, for the funeral. Maybe he'd even see Al there. And then again, maybe not. According to the Millers, Al was very bitter. With good cause, certainly.

Well, Aunt Francie would be here this evening, and tomorrow his father. There seemed to be sound reason

187

in the holding of funerals: everyone came to try to console you. Only he didn't really need consoling. He had lost nothing that had ever been his, and on account of the loss he felt nothing now. Just sordidness. Guilt. And no one could help him with that except himself.

When he pulled into the drive he saw that Jeannie must be home. Her car was there, and another. He was glad someone else would be there. To see her alone was too much of a strain. Something might break, as it had on the boat when he'd forgotten everything and kissed her. He mustn't let that happen again. Jeannie deserved something better than what he could offer her.

When she looked up from her seat at the desk and saw Harry she knew at once he'd heard every word she had said to Quint. That Betty had been murdered; that she had left a note.

She hadn't had time to tell Quint who it was. She hadn't time now. She had said at once, stupidly, "Oh, it's you." And now before she could call for help or say his name, Harry's hand closed over hers on the phone and forced it down on its cradle.

"Lucky I came by, isn't it?" He studied her with obvious dislike. "Now, you smart bitch, where's this message?" She just looked at him.

His eyes swerved to the desk and focused on the phone pad. *"That?"* He bent closer and made out the squiggles that looked different from the rest. "Um. That's shorthand, isn't it?"

She didn't answer and he struck her across the face. She gave a little cry but still said nothing. Her hands gripped the arms of the desk chair as she glared up at him.

"Oh, one of those gutsy ones, are you? Only not the right kind of gutsy or you and I would have been friends long ago. Damn little Puritan, aren't you!"

He bent and looked more closely at the pad. "What's it say?"

"It says 'Harry Judge killed.' "

"Well I'll be damned! That clever little slut!" Viciously he yanked the page off the pad, along with the next two or three under it and stuffed them all in his pocket. "Lucky the cops missed it. I guess they weren't hunting for other messages after they found the suicide note. And it's a good thing I came back; I knew I should take another look around." His eyes traveled slowly over the walls and the furnishings, looking carefully to be sure he hadn't missed anything else. Jeannie took advantage of the moment to slip from the chair where he had kept her penned and move behind it.

"You *did* kill her—didn't you!" She heard her own voice, surprisingly clear and steady, accusing him.

"That," he said, "is something you are never going to be able to tell anyone about."

189

She had always known that Harry was mean; he had treated Karen very badly. But she had never seen him look as he did now. It wasn't pretty. He hates me, she thought to herself; and not just because I've found him out—he's always hated me.

"Shorthand!" As he said it his lip curled. "If it weren't for you no one would ever have known. Just as no one knew about the others—except Betty, of course. She knew."

"Betty knew what?"

"About Old Man Kendrick. And the old harpy." He almost threw the information at her, as if to terrify her with a list of his victims, render her helpless with fear.

"You killed Mr. Kendrick?"

"Why, yes; it wasn't the train wreck at all. I bashed in his head with a piece of broken metal I found in the aisle." With his bright eyes he watched her, expecting her to cringe away. "Betty was sitting right across from me that day . . ."

He was moving towards her now, almost imperceptibly, alert, ready to pounce if she should try to break away.

Jeannie moistened her lips. "And Mrs. Wiebald, why her?"

"She got in my way, that's all. When I was trying to run down Betty with the Jaguar." He might have been describing a move at chess.

And I'm in your way now, Jeannie thought.

She edged to one side—just a slight movement but it was enough to put Harry into action. He grabbed her arm and swung her around. She kicked him and broke loose, but before she could reach the door he had caught her again. She screamed.

"Stop that!" His voice was sharp with anger. He got her by the throat. She kicked, but he held on. Uselessly, her fingers tore at his hands. The room, even Harry's face, so close to hers, began to go black.

Then suddenly she was released. Dimly, as through a gray veil interposed between her and the room, she saw Tom as he struck Harry with his fist—once and then again. From outside the sound of a siren penetrated, urgent, coming with help.

Harry turned and ran, and Tom went after him.

Harry was in the drive by the time Tom reached the front steps. Scrambling into his car he tried hurriedly to start the engine, but before he could get it to turn over Tom had followed him and wrenched open the door. Down the long drive sped two police cars, their red flasher lights revolving and sirens whining. They screeched to a halt on either side of Harry's car and before Tom had had time to haul him out from behind the steering wheel, Tom was grabbed from behind, Harry was pulled out of the car and held firmly by an officer on either side, and Captain Fellini was wanting to know what went on.

Together Tom and the captain went into the house

where Tom strode ahead to the den. Jeannie had sunk down on the leather couch. Her mouth was bleeding, her fingers were pressed tight against her temples, and her eyes were closed. They flew open as Tom bent over her. He took both her hands in his and sat down beside her.

"Harry Judge attacked you?" Captain Fellini asked her.

"Yes. He tried to choke me. But first he admitted killing Betty Graham. Also Mrs. Wiebald. And he killed Mr. Kendrick, on the train—it *wasn't* the train wreck as everyone thought."

"Really? Just a minute." The captain left them quite suddenly, perhaps to take another look at such an interesting prisoner and tighten the guard.

"You all right?" Tom asked.

Jeannie nodded. She looked down at his hands holding hers and smiled. "That's what you said before."

"Before what?"

"Before you kissed me before."

He kissed her. And it was all right now. Whatever had held him in its frozen grip had broken, and the feeling came flooding back.

When Quint got there he stood quite unnoticed in the doorway to the den until he cleared his throat.

"Well," he said, "it doesn't look to me as if either of you is in any need of counsel."